PRAISE FOR

Here are some of the ov......views left for the Dead Cold Mystery series.

"Rex Stout and Michael Connelly have spawned a protege."

AMAZON REVIEW

"So begins one damned fine read."

AMAZON REVIEW

"Mystery that's more brain than brawn."

AMAZON REVIEW

"I read so many of this genre...and ever so often I strike gold!"

AMAZON REVIEW

"This book is filled with action, intrigue, espionage, and everything else lovers of a good thriller want."

AMAZON REVIEW

LITTLE DEAD RIDING HOOD

A DEAD COLD MYSTERY

BLAKE BANNER

RIGHTHOUSE

Copyright © 2024 by Right House

All rights reserved.

The characters and events portrayed in this ebook are fictitious. Any similarity to real persons, living or dead, is coincidental and not intended by the author.

No part of this book may be reproduced in any form or by any electronic or mechanical means, including information storage and retrieval systems, without written permission from the author, except for the use of brief quotations in a book review.

ISBN-13: 978-1-63696-013-5

ISBN-10: 1-63696-013-8

Cover design by: Damonza

Printed in the United States of America

www.righthouse.com

www.instagram.com/righthousebooks

www.facebook.com/righthousebooks

twitter.com/righthousebooks

DEAD COLD MYSTERY SERIES
An Ace and a Pair (Book 1)
Two Bare Arms (Book 2)
Garden of the Damned (Book 3)
Let Us Prey (Book 4)
The Sins of the Father (Book 5)
Strange and Sinister Path (Book 6)
The Heart to Kill (Book 7)
Unnatural Murder (Book 8)
Fire from Heaven (Book 9)
To Kill Upon A Kiss (Book 10)
Murder Most Scottish (Book 11)
The Butcher of Whitechapel (Book 12)
Little Dead Riding Hood (Book 13)
Trick or Treat (Book 14)
Blood Into Wine (Book 15)
Jack In The Box (Book 16)
The Fall Moon (Book 17)
Blood In Babylon (Book 18)
Death In Dexter (Book 19)
Mustang Sally (Book 20)
A Christmas Killing (Book 21)
Mommy's Little Killer (Book 22)
Bleed Out (Book 23)

[Dead and Buried (Book 24)](#)
[In Hot Blood (Book 25)](#)
[Fallen Angels (Book 26)](#)
[Knife Edge (Book 27)](#)
[Along Came A Spider (Book 28)](#)
[Cold Blood (Book 29)](#)
[Curtain Call (Book 30)](#)

ONE

"Family." He said it as though it was the answer to a particularly complicated equation. Then he smiled, like he expected me to be amazed at that answer, and turned his smile on Dehan, pulling up his bedclothes as he did so. Rain rattled on the windowpane. A dull, wet glow highlighted his left profile, leaving the right side of his face in semidarkness. He didn't want the lights on. His eyes were too sensitive. There was a smell of encroaching death in the room. I had the feeling it was lying patiently in the corners and in the shadows, waiting to creep forward when nobody was looking. It was the reek of flavorless food, musty clothes, and too much disinfectant. I had a strong urge to get up and leave. My attention strayed through the rain-spattered glass to the sodden lawn. A drip from the eaves sounded like an accelerated clock.

Sean Reynolds was talking again. "Everybody thinks family is an Italian thing." He pronounced it "eye-talian." "Like the Italians invented family. 'Family.'" He wheezed a laugh. "You gotta say it like you're Robert De Niro. But I'm Irish. I'm not Italian. We came over two centuries ago. And let me tell you, family is just as important to an Irishman as it is to any Italian."

Dehan was sitting in a sage-green armchair that looked almost black in the failing light. She said, "Mr. Reynolds, we were told that your son, Samuel, had some new evidence for us . . ."

"Oh, he has, he won't be long. He's only gone down in the truck to the store. There are things I need, you know. He's a good lad. He brought my bed down to the living room, so's I wouldn't have to climb the stairs. I'm practically bedridden. Family, see? He never married, stayed here with me and Hen."

"Hen?"

"Helen. We call her Hen. Always have. She's not . . ." He screwed up his face, made a gesture with his finger going around in circles at his temple, and mouthed, "*not all there* . . . We've had some family tragedies. If I told you, believe me."

Dehan nodded. "That's the girl who let us in?"

"Hen, yeah."

"And where is she now? Does she know anything about this new evidence . . . ?"

"Up in her room. She stays in her room. She's on medication. She didn't used to take it, but now Samuel makes sure she takes it. He's a good lad. I don't know . . ." He said this last as though answering an inaudible query, then shook his head slowly on the pillow and repeated, "I don't know . . ." Then, after a long pause gazing at the rain outside, he added, "What we'd do without him."

I looked at my watch and drew breath to say that maybe we could come back some other time, but his eyes were glazed and his mind was somewhere else. "Since Eileen died," he said, in that way he had of making statements as though they were related to something nobody had said.

Dehan spoke from the shadows of her chair. "Eileen was your wife."

It wasn't a question, and he didn't answer, he just kept staring at the window, with his mouth slightly open and the covers pulled up almost to his chin.

"Giving birth to Celeste," he said.

"So Celeste never knew her mother?"

He gave his head the most imperceptible shake. "The good Lord gave us Celeste and took away her mother, all on the same night, twenty years ago, on November ninth. Samuel was only six years old. Helen was eight, and poor Celeste came into the world without ever knowing her mom. That was a cruel night." His gaze drifted from the window to rest on Dehan's face. His smile made him look somehow older than he was. He couldn't have been more than sixty-five, but lying there, he might have been a hundred. "We pulled together, as family. I think Samuel realized that night that it was up to him and me to pull through. To pull the family through."

A flurry of wind dragged wet leaves across the patch of lawn visible through the glass. The air seemed to groan through the house, and I heard the front door open and close. Big feet tramped past. We sat in silence and listened to a fridge open and close three times, cupboard doors bang, then big feet tramped back and the door to the room opened.

Samuel occupied the whole doorway. The hall behind him was as dark and gloomy as the room in front of him. He narrowed his eyes to observe Dehan, and then me, where I sat at the foot of the old man's bed. He had an angry face, like it had been cast that way, and he'd look mad whatever mood he was in. His narrowed eyes now made him look angrier. His voice was surprisingly quiet.

"I'm sorry I'm late," he said. "I had to get some things."

I stood and showed him my badge. "Mr. Reynolds, I am Detective John Stone. This is Detective Carmen Dehan." She stood also and showed him her badge. "We run the cold-cases unit at the Forty-Third. We got a message that you have some new evidence relating to a cold case."

He didn't look at our badges. He listened to me, and when I had finished, he went over to his father. "How are you doing, Daddy?" he said. "Will I make you your cocoa?"

My voice was a little louder than I had intended. I sighed and said, "Mr. Reynolds, we are very busy and we can't afford to spend the afternoon sitting around waiting for you. If you have something to tell us, then we would appreciate you doing it now."

He stood erect and scowled at me. "He always has his cocoa at this time."

I pulled a card from my wallet and handed it to him. "When you're ready, call me and come down to the station house."

The old man was flapping his hands. "Sit down, sit down. Samuel, you can't keep the police waiting on you, I'll have my cocoa later. Sit down."

Samuel hesitated a moment, then pulled over a straight-backed chair and sat by the window with the cold, silver light on his face. We sat too, and Dehan pulled a notebook from her pocket.

I said, "Samuel, we got your message and came straight over. We haven't looked at the file yet. So if you could fill us in a little, that would help."

He didn't answer straightaway. When he did, he said, "I asked for Lenny. Lenny had the case."

"Lenny Davis?"

He nodded.

"Detective Davis doesn't work cold cases. Like I said, we run the cold-cases unit. This case is two years old now."

Dehan was making notes. "Don't worry, we'll be sure and talk to him to get us up to speed."

His back was very straight, and he had his big hands on his knees. His trousers were a rusty corduroy. His sweater was a darker rust color, like his tightly curled hair. He wet his lips with his tongue. "I went to see Chad."

Dehan sighed. "Who's Chad?"

"Chad Norris was Celeste's boyfriend, kind of. She was seeing him, used to stay over with him. I always thought he was the one who killed her. I didn't like her seeing him. That's where she was going the night she was killed. To see him."

"Celeste," I said, "was your younger sister. She was eighteen at the time, and you didn't approve of her boyfriend, Chad."

He gave a single nod.

"What was it about him, Samuel, that you didn't like?"

"He was one of those, you know, like he thought he was superior. His dad's got lots of money, and he has his own house his dad bought for him, and he's studying law, going to be a big shot lawyer, you know. Like he was too good for us."

Dehan scratched her head and leaned back in her chair, crossing one long leg over the other. "If he was going out with your sister, how could he think he was too good for you?"

There was a resentful glaze to his eyes now, and a slight curl of the lip. "Well, she was getting ideas herself. Maybe she thought she was too good for us too."

"Samuel!" Sean, the old man, had got up on one elbow. The aged weakness had evaporated from his face. In its place, there was a scowl that instantly cowed his son. "Family! That's your sister!"

I studied the old man's face as he sank back into the pillows, and the appearance of sickness seeped back into the folds and creases. I glanced at Samuel. He was rubbing his palm with his thumb. "So what made you think Chad killed your sister?"

He shrugged. "She was going to his house that night. Probably going to stay the night. She did often enough."

I waited, but there was nothing more. "Forgive me for insisting, Samuel, but going to visit somebody isn't normally a motive for murder. There has to be something more."

"Well, it's him. He's a violent sort, aggressive. He used to attack her..."

Dehan looked up from her pad. "Physically?"

"No... well... She said he used to push her if he got mad. He had a temper. He'd pinch her sometimes too. But mostly it was verbal. He used to humiliate her, shout at her. She told me about it and it made her cry. It made me mad. I told her I'd go talk to him, but she said not to. Like she didn't want him to meet us. Like she was ashamed of us."

"So you never met him?"

"Never till now."

"He lives near here?"

It was his father who answered. "Croes Avenue, not more than five or ten minutes' walk down Gleason." And he told us the number.

I said, "So, what happened that night?"

Samuel said to his hand, "I would have thought you'd know that. Lenny would have known. That's why I thought they'd send him."

I smiled as amiably as I could, though he wasn't looking at me, and in that gloom he probably wouldn't have seen me anyway.

"As I said, Samuel, we were only just handed the case, and we haven't had a chance yet to study the file. What happened that night?"

Again it was his father who answered for Samuel. He was smiling and seemed to be talking to Dehan. "She'd never known her mother. She never had a mother figure, to show her the way. She was my good girl though, hey, Samuel? Lovely, sweet-natured child, couldn't do enough to help around the house. Always obedient and polite."

Samuel was nodding, still rubbing the palm of his hand, like he had a stain there he was trying to remove.

The old man frowned. "But as she got older, the lack of maternal guidance began to tell a little. Samuel and I . . ." He looked over at me as though I would be better equipped to understand the next bit. "We weren't best suited, being men, you know? When she became a woman, we didn't really know . . . how to guide her and that."

Samuel finally looked up from his hand at his father. "We did the best we could, Daddy. But . . ." He looked frankly at Dehan. "No offense, but women can be real hard to understand sometimes. Especially at the time of the month. It's like two out of every five weeks, some women go crazy."

Dehan gave a bark of laughter. "You're not kidding. But don't let the thought police hear you say that."

He gave a small frown like he didn't know what she was talking about. "Anyway, by the time Celeste was sixteen, it seemed she was going to be one of those. She started going out a lot with boys, staying out late, drinking. You know the sort of thing."

His dad was scowling at the floor. "She wasn't a whore!" he said suddenly. "She was a good girl. But when she hit her teens, she went a bit wild. Maybe it was her Irish blood. God knows I was no saint at sixteen—nor at twenty-six! It took your blessed mother to make me settle down. Lord! I miss that woman every day of my life! She would have known how to calm Celeste. She would have known how to talk to her, how to make her see sense. God must know in his wisdom why he had to take her from us, but it nearly killed me when he did. And I believe it killed Celeste."

Dehan frowned. "How's that, Mr. Reynolds?"

"If she had still been with us, Celeste would not have been so wild, I'm sure of it. She would not have been out that night, and if she had, she would have been with a nicer type of man."

"So you also believe Chad might have been responsible for her death?"

"If not him, one like him. They're all the same, boozing, taking drugs, having their damned parties."

Dehan spoke suddenly, "Okay, so, let me see if I've got this straight. Sunday, the sixth of November, she goes out, at night, to walk to Chad's house, five or ten minutes down the road?"

Samuel nodded.

"Okay, so where had she been that weekend?"

"She had spent most of Friday and all of Saturday with him, stayed the night, and came back lunchtime on Sunday." He said all this flatly, without looking at us, in a voice made mechanical by shame.

I asked, "How was she when she got in? Was she her normal self? Did she seem preoccupied?"

Neither of them answered.

I said, "Well?"

The old man said, "You have to remember, Detective, that without a mother to intercede, communication wasn't always easy. Me and Samuel, we can talk to each other, we understand each other, but with Celeste, at that time, she could be sullen."

Samuel said, "And I was angry with her for staying out, so we had words in the kitchen. Daddy come in to sort it out, and the two of us wound up shouting at Celeste, and her shouting back . . ."

"Samuel!"

"Well, they have to know, Daddy! That's how it was. It's nobody's fault! But she wound up storming up the stairs to her room, slamming the door, and not coming out."

Dehan said, "Until?"

The old man answered. "I'll never forget it so long as I live. Eight thirty p.m., she come down those stairs, in her torn jeans, big, black boots like a soldier's boots, her hair—she had lovely, wild red hair—her hair all scrunched under a woolen cap, and a dirty, big, red woolen jacket with a hood. You know, I often think what a tragedy, such a beautiful girl—and she was lovely looking, wasn't she, Samuel?—to die looking so bloody awful. I know that sounds like a shallow thing to say, but it's true all the same." His gaze wandered again, out the window. "Such a lovely girl, to die looking like a tramp. When she had her home and her family to care for her."

"So when she came down the stairs, did she say anything?"

Samuel said, "I asked her where she was going, she gave me a mouthful of abuse and said she was going to see Chad. She said at least she felt welcome there."

"And she left?"

"Maybe more things were said. I went to the kitchen. Daddy was begging her to see sense. She walked out and slammed the door behind her."

His daddy had started to sob. He had a big, boney hand over his face and he was making ugly, visceral noises.

Samuel said, "He has angina and high blood pressure. This isn't good for him."

The old man uncovered his face and reached out to us with his other hand. His face was wet and twisted with grief. "I don't want you to go! I want to help! I want to hear what you talk about. It's been two years waiting and I swear it's killing me. I need to hear what you say and what you think . . . Don't go."

I studied him a moment. "We won't keep you much longer, Mr. Reynolds. Just a couple more questions. After Celeste left that night, none of you heard from her again?"

He started sobbing again and Samuel said, "No. Not till the police—well, Lenny—told us she'd been found, down by the river."

I looked at Samuel. "You said you had new evidence, Samuel."

His expression didn't change, but he drew himself up, and there was a challenge in his eyes. "I got tired of waiting for nothing to happen, and I went and talked to Chad."

"When was this?"

"This morning. I told him I thought he'd killed Celeste. He said I was crazy and I ought to be careful making that kind of accusation. Threatened me with all his lawyer talk. I told him I wasn't scared and maybe we should have the whole thing aired in court. He said I was probably stupid enough to do that, and I said that maybe I was. That was when he told me."

"Told you what, Samuel?"

"That she was seeing other men. He said they were both getting tired of each other. He was finding her boring, he said. That they were never serious about having a future together, and that she was seeing at least one other man."

"How did he know that?"

"He said he caught her sending text messages to some guy."

"Did he know these men?"

He shook his head. "He said he didn't. But I reckon he killed her 'cause he was jealous, and now he's just covering up, pretending he don't care. I'll tell you something, he has a wild temper. He can get real mad."

I sighed and glanced at Dehan. She gave me a nod. I said, "Okay, I think what we need to do now is go and study the file, and we may need to get back to you again after that. Do you still have Celeste's things?"

Her father said, "Her room is just as it was the day she left. We haven't had the heart to do anything with it."

"We may need to go through her things at some point, so if you can just keep that room locked for now." I looked at Dehan and we both stood.

The old man said, "You should talk to Lenny. He knows all about it."

"You and Lenny friends?"

He nodded. "Sure. We go back a long way. We grew up in the same street. I was older than him, taught him his way around." He laughed. "Ask him. He'll tell you. 'You know old Sean Reynolds?' He'll know."

I smiled. "I'll be sure to talk to him."

Samuel let us out onto Beach Avenue and closed the door behind us. I noticed a cream Toyota pickup truck parked outside the gate. The rain had stopped, but odd, icy drops were still falling from fat, low-slung gray clouds, propelled by sporadic gusts of wind. We walked in silence toward my old, burgundy Jaguar. Rusty, wet leaves had gathered in drifts around its spoked wheels and, though it was only five in the afternoon, the lights were coming on in the windows down the street, and headlamps were reflecting wet across the blacktop.

As Dehan stood by the passenger door, she asked me, "You want to grab some coffee and pull the file?"

I nodded like I was agreeing, because my mind was on something else. Then I shook it and said, "No, I already pulled the file. It's on the back seat. I want to take a five- or ten-minute walk down Gleason Avenue and have a chat with Chad. I think we should see just how formidable his temper really is."

TWO

We walked among the eclectic jumble of clapboard and red brick that is Gleason Avenue, with the cold, desultory breeze creeping around our ankles and feeling its way into gaps and openings in our coats and sleeves. Heavy traffic, homeward bound, hissed over wet asphalt, or waited rumbling in long lines at the traffic lights, which gleamed off shiny, wet chassis and lay like spilled, luminous liquid among the puddles.

We went three blocks and came to the Watson Gleason Playground, skirted on all four sides by giant chestnut trees. Opposite the entrance to the playground, there was a large, redbrick building. On the corner there was a grocery store, and above it apartments. I pointed at the windows and said, "The only witness Lenny could find lived in that apartment up there."

Dehan looked surprised. "How do you know?"

"When I pulled the file, I had a quick read."

"Why didn't you tell me?"

"You were getting coffee. I didn't want to distract you."

"Jerk."

We dodged through the traffic and I rang on the bell beside a bright, red door. Dehan was still making a question at me with her face. I smiled. "You were talking to the inspector. I found the file, leafed through it, and had a quick look, happened to notice there was only one witness. Don't get touchy."

"Don't cut me out." She poked me on the chest. "You know it makes me mad."

The door opened to reveal a plump woman in her late twenties or early thirties. She had thick, black hair in a big halo around her head and huge brown eyes that were itching to laugh. She seemed to be dressed in amorphous brown cloth bags and leaned on the doorjamb chewing gum.

"You cops? I was just going to the store." She made it sound like "sto-wa."

I smiled back at her eyes and that made her grin. "We won't keep you. Are you Remedios Borja?"

"Not if you're gonna arrest me."

"We're not."

"Then that's me. You got me." She laughed as though she'd made a joke.

Dehan made a strange face that should have been a smile but wasn't and said, "Do you remember a couple of years back, you made a statement to the police? It was a murder investigation?"

"Uh-huh. But I don't remember much. It's rained a lot since then, right?"

I gave her a warm smile, which made her grin again. "Just tell us what you saw."

She shrugged. "Not a lot." She pointed across the road. "It was like nine o'clock, maybe a bit earlier. It was dark. I'd left the drapes open. It was around this time of year, November. It was cold. I dunno, I guess I'd been in the kitchen, whatever, I left the drapes open. So I went to close them. And when I did, I saw this girl just, like, standing, right over there on the corner, near the tree."

She pointed at the giant chestnut outside the gate to the playground. We both turned to look. I said, "She was just standing there?"

"Uh-huh. I thought at first she was a whore, and that made

me mad 'cause we don't get whores around here. This is a nice neighborhood. But then I thought she didn't really look like a hooker. Her clothes, her hair. She looked a mess."

"Can you remember how she was dressed?"

"Oh sure. I wouldn't forget that. It wasn't raining, but it was kind of drizzling? And she had on this big-ass old red jacket. I think it was a couple of sizes too big for her, with the hood over her head. And she was standing, with her hands in her pockets . . ."

I asked, "Which way was she facing, Remedios?"

"Oh, she was facing down toward White Plains . . ."

"East."

She grinned. "If you say so. Anyhow, next thing I see, there's a guy there, and they are talkin' and he seems to be mad. She looks pretty mad too."

Dehan said, "Can you describe him?"

"He was tall, taller than her, anyhow. Big. He had a leather jacket, I think, and one of them woolen hats that roll down? Can't say more than that."

I said, "What happened next?"

"Next thing, she's shouting at him. We got triple glazing, so I couldn't hear what she was saying. But he grabs her shoulders and starts kind'a shaking her. She slaps him and she turns and disappears behind that big tree there . . ." She pointed at the second giant chestnut. "After that, I lost sight of them and closed the drapes."

I frowned. "Did you see if he went after her?"

"Oh, for sure. He definitely went after her. He was kind of half running and reaching out for her."

Dehan shook her head. "You didn't think to call the cops?"

Remedios rolled her eyes. "Don't give me no lecture, sister. If I called the cops every time I see a boy put his hand on a girl, or a girl give a boy some attitude, this place would be crawlin' with cops twenty-four fockin' seven. I called the cops when I read about the girl in the river, with the big red coat. You feel me?"

I said, "Yeah, we feel you. Did anybody else see anything?"

"Nobody talked to me about it."

"Okay, thanks, Remedios. You've been very helpful."

"Sure, anytime."

She watched us cross the road through the traffic again and continue west toward Croes Avenue.

Dehan fell into step beside me, watching her boots as she trod the wet sidewalk. She spoke to no one in particular, simply voicing her thoughts.

"So she spends most of Friday and Saturday with Chad. The whole day and the night. She comes home Sunday midday. She and Samuel get into a big row in the kitchen and Dad comes in to break it up, but winds up joining Samuel in giving Celeste a piece of his mind." She looked up at me. "Have you noticed how Samuel calls his dad Daddy? Is that weird?"

I nodded, but I didn't say anything.

She added, "Especially when they talk so much about family. It's like he never grew up and became a man. Am I being judgmental?"

"Probably, but I know what you mean. Keep going, she gets mad and storms upstairs," I said. "We don't know what she does up there, but she doesn't come down for a few hours."

"Sometime between half past eight and nine o'clock. One thing stands out a mile. She was sick of her father and Samuel, and Samuel had had about a bellyful of her. And I think that goes for her dad too. He makes a big show of not criticizing her, but privately, I am pretty sure he and Samuel had both had about as much of her as they could swallow."

I looked at her curiously. "Are you suggesting Samuel killed his sister?"

She stuck out her bottom lip and shoved her hands in her back pockets, then looked up into my face. "No . . . not necessarily. But I sure as hell wouldn't rule him out." She shrugged. "Five, ten minutes after she walked out of the house, she stops at the playground to wait for somebody. A guy who could fit Samuel's description turns up and they have a row. She tries to walk away, and he goes after her. Next time anybody sees Celeste, she's dead, washed up on the banks of the Bronx River. And . . ." She half turned back the way we'd come. "She was waiting, looking back the way she'd come."

"So you think, what? That Samuel phoned her, told her to wait for him, and came after her to continue their row?"

"It's not an impossible scenario."

"No, it's not impossible, but is it likely she would stand waiting for him to continue a row she has just walked out on twice before?"

She grunted.

I pointed up ahead. We were approaching a twenty-story tower block on the right. "This is it, here on the left."

Chad's house was an ugly, flat, redbrick construction with four sash windows on the upper floor and four concrete steps behind an iron railing and gate leading up to a white front door.

Dehan went in ahead of me and rang the bell, but by that time we could already hear the shouting inside. She had to ring three times and eventually hammer on the wood before thumping feet approached and the door was wrenched open. The guy who wrenched it open was probably twenty-five with expensively cut blond hair, pale blue eyes, and a face that was cruelly handsome. He was slim, in Levi's jeans and a Columbia University sweatshirt. His eyes flicked over Dehan, then over me, and he said, "What?"

She showed him her badge and I showed him mine.

"I'm Detective Carmen Dehan. This is my partner, Detective John Stone. Are you Chad Norris?"

"Yeah. Why?"

"We'd like to talk to you about Celeste Reynolds."

He gave a small sigh through his nose. He gazed at the wall, chewing his lip, then he stared at the corner of the door. He put his hands on his hips and stepped away from us, then turned back. "You know, I'm just wondering," he said, "what could you do—no, seriously—what could you do to make my day any *fucking worse*? No, I mean it, go ahead, do it! I mean, my roommate just broke my *damned television*! I tell him to leave *and he starts crying like a fucking girl*!" He stared up the stairs, as though he wanted to see if his roommate could hear him. "*Can you hear me? You fucking pussy!*"

I said, "Mr. Norris, unfortunately, we haven't got time to wait for you to grow up. If you can't talk to us now, then perhaps you could come down to the station, but one way or another, we need to talk to you."

He came down the stairs again and walked toward us, jerking out his knees and blinking. "I'm sorry. You haven't got time for *what*?"

I watched him with interest.

He said again, "You haven't got time for *what*?"

Dehan looked up at me. "Would you say his manner was threatening, Stone? He looks out of control to me." Before I could answer, she had turned back to him. "Sir, have you been consuming drugs or alcohol? Have you got drugs or alcohol on the premises? You seem to me to be out of control and somewhat threatening in your manner."

Suddenly, Chad Norris was smiling. His hands were up and he was laughing. "Whoa, whoa, whoa! Take it easy there, tiger! Okay, okay, why don't we start again without the attitude. I was mad. I apologize. I was certainly *not* threatening you in any way!" With a touch of sarcasm, he gestured us inside with both hands, like a waiter guiding us to a table. "How about you come in, and, please, tell me how I can help you?"

I gave him a humorless smile. "Yeah, how about that?"

The house looked newly decorated. A broad, light hallway with polished wooden floors was laid with a cream carpet that climbed a staircase to the upper floor. The banisters and the walls were also painted cream, and on the left a bare pine door stood open onto a room with white calico sofas and armchairs. Chad made for the stairs with an unpleasant smile on his face.

"Go right on in. I'll be with you in a moment. I just need to deal with something upstairs."

The room was dominated by a vast, black, flat-screen TV on a stand. Aside from the sofa and the chair, there was practically no furniture, except for a coffee table piled with magazines and books on law. French doors stood closed, spattered with rain in the failing light, offering a view of an unkempt backyard with an overgrown lawn. Pretty soon, we heard Chad's voice hollering upstairs:

"*You get the fuck out of my house! I don't give a damn what you do. Just get out! You have fifteen minutes to get your shit together and get out!*"

A door slammed and feet thumped down the stairs. Chad entered the room and stopped, smiling at us both in turn. "Sometimes you just have to tell it how it is. Then you feel better." He gestured at the sofa with both hands. "Sit."

He sat. Dehan sat in the corner of the sofa. I remained standing by the French doors.

"You want to talk to me about Celeste."

Dehan answered, "We're from the cold-cases unit at the Forty-Third."

"You guys have one of those? I thought that was just on TV." His smile was amiable, but there was no hiding the sarcasm in his eyes. Dehan carried on as though he hadn't spoken.

"We're reviewing Celeste's case, and we understand that you two were pretty close."

He nodded at her, still smiling amiably. "What of it?"

Dehan raised an eyebrow. "That's it? 'What of it?' That's your reply?"

He gave a small laugh. "Forgive me, perhaps it's all the browbeating we get at Columbia: 'Be precise! Be precise! What, exactly, are you saying?' But I am not clear exactly what you are asking me. You are correct. Celeste and I were, at one time, close."

Dehan sat forward with her elbows on her knees and took a

moment to study the backs of her fingers. "I hadn't got around to asking you any questions yet, Chad, but when I do, I promise you they will be very precise." Now she raised her eyes to meet his. "Working on the assumption that you want us to find your girlfriend's killer, I was inviting you to engage with us and share information."

"Oh, well, now, see, she wasn't exactly my girlfriend. We were more like friends with benefits."

"Not much of a benefit to her."

He shrugged and spread his hands. "What do you want me to say? Her getting killed had nothing to do with being my friend."

"Well that's not exactly true, is it, Chad?" She was studying the backs of her long fingers again. "Because she was on her way to see you when she disappeared."

He gave his head a quick shake. "Oh, but you don't know that for a fact, do you?"

I laughed. "What's that thing you guys are so fond of quoting? 'The truth is a philosophical concept. Fact is something you can prove in court.' Well, we know for a fact that she was on her way to see you when she was last seen alive. Now, we have a lot of very precise questions that we would like to ask about that. Like, did she ever get here? What happened when she did? But right now what we would prefer, Chad, is for you to drop the Ivy League attorney act and make like you give a damn that she was killed. Tell us about that weekend."

He gaped at me for a while, then blinked and readjusted his ass on the chair. "Well, *of course* I give a damn. But, you know, it was two years ago. You have to move on, right? But I was really cut up about her death. Ask any one of my friends!"

Dehan smiled sweetly at him. "You have any left from back then?"

He swallowed. His face said he was wondering if he had.

I said, "Just tell us about that weekend, Chad. Try to stick to the truth. I mean the philosophical concept. It has a way of coming out and biting you in the ass if you ignore it."

I moved and sat on the sofa, and he started to talk.

THREE

"You have to understand that one thing I do not have is time. Law at Columbia is a total commitment. And the people who do not commit fail. It is that simple. Commitment is the baseline, it's what you do on top of commitment that makes you a winner. And what you do on top is sacrifice things that other people take for granted as a normal part of life: parties, girlfriends, evenings in front of the TV, chilling, eating pizza . . . All that will come, and more. But right now—and back then—it is focus, focus, focus. My dad summed it up for me when I was a kid, and I always remember what he said. 'Focus is commitment, and commitment is focus.'

"So there is only one way you can have a girlfriend in a situation like this. It's like the Clintons. She wasn't just helping him and supporting him, she was there doing it with him. But how many women are there with the focus and drive of Hillary? Right?"

The question was directed at me, but then he looked at Dehan and said, "No offense."

"None taken. Believe me."

"So I have no time for a romantic attachment. I have needs, like all guys, but I can't commit to a woman. So along comes

Celeste. I can't even remember where we met. It was at a club. One of the rare occasions when I went out. She was there and hunting for a guy, and a mutual acquaintance introduced us."

Dehan was shaking her head. "Wait a minute. Hunting for a guy? What does that mean?"

He shrugged and made a face. "You know! Girls like Celeste, they have no money, but they want a good time, so they hang around clubs where guys with money go and they hunt. Sometimes they hunt in packs, sometimes they go solo. They find a guy who looks like he has money and they close in. Maybe it's a one-night stand, maybe it develops into a long-term solution for their lives.

"So she was cute, she was kind of wild, we had fun, and I told her, in the morning, I don't do this. I am not a party guy. I am focused on my career and nothing is going to get in the way of that." He laughed. "Well, it had the opposite effect from what I had intended. It was like music to her ears, man. I kept telling her, look, we are just friends with benefits. I am not going to marry you. When I marry, it will be the daughter of some CEO, and there will be a prenup that ensures if we ever divorce, I will come out of it a rich man. Sorry!" He hunched his shoulders in a way that said he really wasn't. "You wanted truth. That's truth. I think at first she didn't believe it, but after a bit, things were not so good between us . . ."

Dehan asked, "What does that mean?"

"She was becoming a bit suffocating." He appealed to me. "You know how chicks can get. She was, like, always around. I was like, 'Don't you have a fucking home to go to?' I mean . . ." He flopped back in the chair and sighed. "I didn't want to kick her out because of the sex, right? But it was becoming a case of diminishing returns. You know? She was becoming boring, and the sex just wasn't so good anymore. So, things were getting a little tense."

I asked, "Were you having rows?"

He shook his head. "Celeste didn't row. If you got mad at

Celeste, she just screamed at you a couple of times and walked away."

"Where'd she go?"

He shrugged and made a face of absolute ignorance. "I have no idea, man. She would just leave the house, but before long, she'd be right back again."

Dehan said, "So what happened that weekend?"

He sat forward, elbows on knees, rubbed his face, and sighed. "She came over in the morning on Friday and stayed the night. You have to understand, Saturday to me is just like any other day. I can't go to the examining board and say, 'Hey, my examination is not up to scratch because I spent the damned weekend with a chick who wanted me to pay attention to her.' 'Oh, okay, Mr. Norris, don't worry, we'll give you an A anyway!' It doesn't happen that way."

"So what happened?"

"I went upstairs to get away from her and Nigel . . ." He froze. His face flushed with anger. "Did he leave yet? Did you hear him leave?"

I raised an eyebrow at him. "Stay focused, Chad. What happened?"

He took a deep breath and bit his lip. "Okay! So I went upstairs to get away from Celeste and Nigel, in my own house, I went upstairs to get away from their *incessant yammering*! And the damned TV! I guess she spent the day here and in the evening I came down, they had opened a bottle of wine, and I had a glass. She goes up to the john and while she's up there, Nigel starts telling me I should know when I am onto a good thing. I am not likely to find a girl as good and loyal as Celeste. She really loves me, I should take more care of her, yadda yadda yadda. Bottom line, if I am not careful, she will find somebody else."

"Was he saying that he was interested in her?"

He burst out laughing. "Nigel? Nah! Nigel is gay. He likes sailors with striped shirts and big moustaches. *Isn't that right, Nigel?*" There was a little gasp from the door, the stamping of feet, and the front door slammed. "Son of a bitch was at the door all along."

I sighed. "So what did he mean, she would find somebody else?"

He nodded several times. "I know, right? She's eating here, she's sleeping here, she's watching my TV, using my utilities, and all the while she's fucking some other guy. So I took her phone and I started looking through the messages. And I see there is this guy . . ." He thought for a moment. "Rod? Rod, yeah, and he is sending her all these messages about how hot she is and how he wants to do this to her and that to her . . ."

Dehan said, "And how was she responding to these messages?"

He stared hard at her, with eyes that were almost calculating. "That was the smart thing, right? She didn't respond in kind. Her replies were all short. But, each one of them had *something* to encourage him. She was enticing him to believe that there could be something between them, if . . ."

"If what?"

"I told you at the start. Chicks like Celeste are predators. They're out hunting for a guy who will solve their problems. If she was going to sleep with him, she wanted something in return. She wasn't a hooker, but she was a whore."

"Did you confront her with the messages?"

"You bet your sweet ass I did!"

She stared at him for a long moment. "Watch your mouth there, Chad. What happened when you told her you'd looked at her phone?"

"At first, she was mad and started screaming at me that I had no right to check her phone. But then when I started reading the stuff this guy had written to her, she started crying and apologizing. I asked her how many other guys she was screwing around with. She said she wasn't screwing around with anybody. It was just this guy, it was a game, she was going to tell him to get lost . . "

I scratched my head. "Chad. You need to explain this to me. You say she was not your girlfriend. You were just friends with benefits. Yet you got mad when you discovered she'd been cheating on you. You have a big bust-up and I'm guessing you kicked her out . . ."

He gave a small laugh and looked down at the carpet. "Not exactly."

"Not exactly? What does that mean?"

He shrugged. "The bust-up was kind of hot, and you know . . . Makeup sex is the best. She spent the night again, we chilled in the morning, and then she went home around midday."

I scratched my Adam's apple for a bit, trying to visualize the scene. It wasn't all that hard. "Did she contact you again during the afternoon?"

"Yeah, she sent me a couple of messages." He shrugged. "You know, the usual stuff, she loved me, that kind of shit."

Dehan said, "What about Rod?"

He shrugged. "What about him?"

"Did she say she was going to dump him? How did you leave that? You were pretty mad at her because of him."

He stared at a couple of walls for a bit, like he was embarrassed. "Yeah, she said she was going to tell him to lay off. She wasn't into him anyway. She'd been kind of stringing him along for a laugh."

"So do you know him? Do you know who he is?"

He shook his head. "Nah, she said he was some guy she knew. I never met him. Anyway, she said she was going to tell him to leave her alone."

I narrowed my eyes and shook my head. "It never occurred to you that this guy might have been the one who killed her?"

His face went a pasty, yellow color. "No . . ."

Dehan stared at me. "Can you believe this guy? Ivy League." She looked back at him. "You seriously expect me to believe that you saw those sexually explicit messages, you saw that she was teasing him and giving him the come-on, and *the night after* you force her to break it off, she disappears, and you didn't connect the dots? You did not see that there was a possible, *probable*, connection between her disappearance and breaking off with this guy!"

He shook his head. "No . . . She stopped coming around. I thought maybe, even though we'd had the makeup, she'd had enough. Maybe it was just over and that was like the grand finale. Plus, I thought maybe she'd hooked up with this guy after all. That can happen. You meet to break up and you end up getting together. I didn't find out she'd been killed for a few weeks. By that time, I'd moved on, man. I didn't really think about it."

"You're a piece of work, Chad. You're a real piece of work. So did she tell you she was coming over Sunday night or not?"

He shook his head. "No, she just sent me a couple of messages in the afternoon saying she loved me. And that was the last I heard from her."

I asked, "Did you answer those messages?"

"Yeah." He looked embarrassed again. "I told her I loved her too."

Dehan gave him a look that might have withered a sequoia. "Don't worry, your secret is safe with us. Nobody will ever know you pretended to be a human being once."

She made a question with her face and showed it to me. Had I any more questions? I shook my head and stood.

"Your father was right, Chad. Focus and commitment are two sides of the same coin. But they aren't the answer to life's problems. The real secret is knowing what to focus on. If you focus on being a cheap shit all your life, then cheap shit is what life is going to give you. Enjoy your evening."

FOUR

We spent the evening reading and digesting what little there was of the original report, and next morning, on the way to the station house, we took a detour to the corner of Colgate Avenue and Lafayette. It had rained heavily during the night and the roads were wet. The semi-wild riverbanks in Soundview Park were saturated and muddy, so we pulled on our rubber boots in the car and headed down the cycle path.

I didn't know what I was hoping to learn from the exercise except, on some intuitive level, I guess I hoped to get a feel for her last few days. To a lot of cops, especially the later generations reared on IT, that might sound like horse manure. Maybe it was. I don't know how the human mind works, but I do know that, with me at least, the whole process of working out who done it, and how, happens in some dark place in my unconscious. And right then, my dark unconscious wanted to have a look at the place where she washed up. So that's what we did.

Dehan had brought the file with her, and some plastic envelopes for the photographs. We stood on the footpath, where it bends and then forks, located the spot on the bank, and counted out sixty paces, going west and slightly north. There, the grass and undergrowth gave way to a small section of stony beach with a boulder at one end, maybe five feet by three. It was up against that boulder that her body had been found. I stood there, ankle-deep in water, with the slight drizzle speckling my face, and looked around. Dehan was watching me, like she was wondering what I was doing. I might have told her, if she'd asked, that I had no idea.

She came a bit closer, looking at the file. "The ME said she was strangled. Bruising to her neck was extensive, so her killer probably had very strong hands. There was no water in her lungs, so she was put in the river postmortem. She was definitely in the water for several days, possibly a week or more. She was probably thrown in upstream someplace."

I nodded at her. "Oh, I am quite sure she wasn't killed here." I stuck my hands in my pockets and looked upstream, toward the construction site and the cold, black ribbon of water that ran beside it. Where had she come from? I said:

"There aren't that many places you can get access to the river up there. At the moment, I can't think of any." I shrugged one-shouldered. The drizzle trickled in through my hair and down my neck. "A corpse, hundred and ten, hundred and twenty pounds, is very hard to move around, even in dry conditions. What have we got up there? Industrial lots, fenced off from the road on one side and from the river on the other. It was raining. Assuming our killer could somehow manage the almost impossible feat of getting the body over those two fences, he now has to maneuver it through wet, slippery, overgrown undergrowth to be able to drop it into the river . . ."

Dehan was watching me and nodding slowly. She added, "Not only that, he must have weighted her down too. Corpses float for a long time before they finally sink. If she was in the water for a week, that means she was weighted down until the current finally broke her free and dragged her here."

I grunted. "That's quite an achievement. All that without getting noticed, picked up on CCTV, or without setting off any alarms." I took a deep breath and sucked my teeth. "What else have we got up there, Dehan?"

"Westchester Avenue Bridge. But that's fenced off too, and there would be a lot of traffic. The risk of being seen and reported would be very high."

"After that, it's the railway and Starlight Park, by the depot on East 177th. But by then, the river is narrow and shallow." I shook my head. "He had to dump her at, or south of, Starlight Park. And I can't, for the life of me, think of a place between there and here where he might have done that without having to get through chain-link fences and dense undergrowth while carrying or dragging a hundredweight of dead body." I looked at her, wiped the drizzle from my eyes, and said, "If I was looking for a place to dump a body, within a short driving distance from the Watson Gleason Playground, I'd come here. What is it, less than a mile and a half?" I gestured upriver. "Why go to all the trouble, and difficulty, of struggling with the body over fences and/or railway lines if he could have brought her here? If he dumps her here, within the week, instead of *showing up* here, she would be out in the East River and nobody would have any idea where it had come from."

She sniffed and wiped her eyes with her sleeve. I began to squelch through the mud back toward the footpath. Dehan fell into step beside me. "That tells us something," she said. "Actually, it tells us a couple of things: the killer is not experienced. He most likely panicked and went for what he saw, for some reason, as the simplest solution. It also tells us it wasn't premeditated. He had not planned out beforehand how he was going to dispose of the body. So the killing was, possibly, an unpremeditated act of rage. Finally, and this is real important, the killer probably has access to the river through his place of work, somewhere between here and Starlight Park, and *that* was what made him go there, instead of the simpler option of coming here."

We had come to the car and I stood, stamping my boots and nodding. "That makes a lot of sense, Dehan, though it raises the question, how did he get her from the playground to his presumed place of work? We need to get onto that right away, but before we do, I want to talk to Lenny about Celeste's phone records. I would have expected them to be in the file." I opened the car and we sat with the doors open, changing out of our rubber boots. I spoke over my shoulder as I laced up my shoes. "It seems pretty obvious to me that she called somebody, or somebody called her, Saturday night. And that somebody was the person who met her at the playground. That's why she was standing, waiting at the corner: she had arranged to meet somebody, or somebody had arranged to meet her. So our first port of call is to see who she spoke to that night on the phone."

We dumped our boots in the trunk. I climbed in behind the wheel, and she got in the passenger seat and slammed the door. As I fired up the engine, she said, "Shouldn't that be whom? '. . . see whom she spoke to that night on the phone.'"

I pulled away up Colgate Avenue. "Nobody likes a wiseass, Dehan."

"I do," she said. "I like you, and you're a wiseass."

"That's different. Tell me, do you like Chad for this?"

She puffed out her cheeks and blew. "Yes and no."

"Okay. Explain."

"On the 'yes' side, you have the fact that he was clearly much more attached to her than he wanted to admit. Maybe because he's trying to play the ruthless New York attorney, maybe because he is trying to please his father, or maybe because he's smart enough to realize that having feelings for her gives him a motive. Whatever his reasons, he had feelings for her."

"It wasn't all an act. He really is like that."

She nodded. "Yeah, I agree. Don't interrupt. Having said that he has feelings for her, I am willing to believe that those feelings run more to possessiveness, dependency, and sexual ownership than tenderness, love, and caring. So their relationship may well have had that toxicity that can make infidelity a very explosive, violent business. He has a lack of compassion, lack of empathy, his nerves are on edge all the time. Add to that his temper, the fact that he becomes violent and abusive at the flip of a switch, and it is not hard to imagine a situation where he could lose control and kill her. Plus, her phone is missing and we have no phone records, so we only have his word for the fact that she didn't call him, or he didn't call her."

She paused, holding her lower lip between her teeth. "On the other hand," she said. "I believed him. I didn't get the impression at any point that he was lying."

I grunted. "Is that because he was telling the truth, or because he wasn't lying?"

She raised an eyebrow at me and said, "What? Who's being a wiseass now? What the hell is that supposed to mean?"

I laughed. "Okay, let's suppose that Sunday night I went out, scored a couple of grams of coke, got off my head, and then went and shot up a club full of cokeheads and dealers."

"You?"

"Yeah. Now let's suppose you are investigating that crime and you want to know everything that happened on Saturday, the day before, and you question me about Saturday. You don't ask me any questions I need to lie about and so your radar doesn't pick up any dishonest vibes from me. I wasn't lying, per se, but I wasn't telling the whole truth either."

"So what are you saying, that if we had questioned him about Sunday night in more detail, he might have started lying?"

I made a face and shrugged. "I'm just saying that you may have had the feeling he wasn't lying because he had nothing to lie about at that stage."

She was quiet for a while. "Do you like him for it?"

"I don't know yet." And after a moment's silence, I added, "I agree with you, it is easy to imagine the situation arising."

We pulled into the parking lot at the 43rd and ducked in out of the rain. While Dehan started the laborious task of finding out what properties and businesses lay along the banks of the Bronx

River between Starlight Park and Soundview Park, I went to look for Lenny. I found him at the coffee dispenser.

"Hey, Stone. What's happening? I never got to congratulate you. Carmen Dehan, huh? I don't think anybody saw that coming."

"Yeah, least of all me. Listen, we just received new information on the Reynolds case. You remember, two years back . . . ?"

He nodded. "Yeah, sure! I knew them personally." He leaned back against the wall and pointed at the machine. "You want a coffee?"

"No, thanks. I just wanted to ask you a couple of things . . ."

"'Cause they got you and Carmen on the cold cases, right?"

"Yeah. That was your case . . ."

"Yeah, me and Pete were called to the scene, and you can imagine how I felt when I saw Celeste. Holy shit! Now I have to tell her dad, like he hasn't had enough heartache in his life. One crazy daughter . . ."

"Helen?"

"Yeah, she's diagnosed as schizophrenic. She's okay while she's taking her meds, but if she comes off them, she is off with the fairies, I'm telling you. Then his wife dies in childbirth. Can you believe that? Family is everything to this guy. And the one consolation he has for his wife's death, he dotes on his daughter Celeste —she's smart, she's pretty—hey! At least he got something in return for losing his wife, right? Well then, capoom! That very daughter goes and gets herself murdered. You know? Where is the fuckin' justice in that? And I have to go and tell him. 'Hey, your daughter Celeste just got murdered.' It was hard, I don't mind telling you."

I nodded. "That's a tough break."

"For him. I get to go home to my lovely wife and my kids. He gets to go home to the Addams Family!"

I smiled. "You know them well?"

"Nah, not really. We grew up on the same street. We didn't hang out, he was a bit older than me, but we used to say hi. We attended the same Catholic church, Blessed Sacrament, it's right there on his doorstep. His wife was real devout, and his son, Samuel, he's devout too. A bit too much for my taste. And me, well, I don't go anymore. My wife does, but I'm lapsed, you know? Too many unanswered questions." He laughed. "I'm a detective, right? I need proof."

"Right. Listen, Lenny, what I wanted to ask you about..."

"Oh, you ain't asked me yet?" He laughed out loud.

I laughed with him and carried on. "About the phone records."

He kept smiling, but his face became serious. "Yeah, what about them?"

"Did you request them?"

"Celeste's phone records? Yeah, of course. She talked to somebody that night and I wanted to know who."

"Right. That's what I thought. But the records aren't in the file."

He frowned at me like I had suddenly started talking in a foreign language. "Her phone records ain't in the file?"

I shook my head. "Uh-uh. Would you have taken the file home with you? Might they be back at your place?"

He made a face that was skeptical. "I'm pretty sure they're not. I'll have a look for you, pal, but if they've gone missing, they haven't gone missing at my house." He sighed. "The company was Verizon, and if I ain't mistaken, they keep records for just one year."

"Can you remember who she called?"

"Sure!" He shrugged. "It was a burner. If I remember, she called the burner, the burner called her once, and then it called her again. That was . . ." He closed his eyes and screwed up his face. "Uh . . . eight, eight thirty, and ten minutes before nine."

I grunted. "Any other calls around that time?"

"It's two years ago, but . . . yeah. Shortly before the last call, she received a call from the landline at home. That was Samuel telling her to come home and stop acting like a diva. And at, I don't remember exactly, about eight forty-five, a short call from Chad, her boyfriend."

"That's really helpful, thanks, Lenny. Try to find the records for me anyway, would you?"

"Sure, no problem."

I left him standing at the coffee machine and went slowly back to our desks. Dehan was chewing on a celery stick and reading from the screen of her laptop. I dropped into my chair and put my feet on the corner of my desk. I stared at Dehan for a while, but she seemed not to notice. I thought about Chad and wondered why he would lie about having called Celeste that night. Had she arranged to go and spend the night with him? Had she then spoken to Rod and decided to spend the night with him, instead? Was it Chad that Remedios had seen from her window, chasing Celeste behind the chestnut tree?

I wondered about other lies people had told too, and wondered what they had to gain from them. I wondered about Samuel, calling Celeste after she had left the house. And I wondered about the Watson Gleason Playground on a cold, wet November night.

I took a small, blue Post-it, screwed it into a small pellet, and threw it at Dehan. She batted it away without averting her eyes from the screen. "What?"

"Let's go back to the playground."

Now she turned and frowned at me. "What for?"

"Because we are going to find witnesses."

"The area was already canvassed two years ago."

"Well . . . yes and no. We'll canvass it again. Come on, Little Grasshopper. The answer to our mystery, if I am not very much mistaken—and I am not—lies in that playground."

She sighed. "See, you're a wiseass, and a pompous wiseass."

"But you like me nonetheless."

I stood, and we went back out into the rain.

FIVE

It was a short drive from Story Avenue up Rosedale to the Watson Gleason Playground. I parked near the corner of Gleason and Croes and we walked back toward the playground. As we walked, I smiled amiably at the light rain that speckled the blacktop while Dehan spoke.

"If ever proof was needed, Stone," she said, with her hands in her pockets, squinting at the odd mix of ugly buildings around us, "that functional is not necessarily beautiful, this stretch of Gleason Avenue is it." I drew breath to answer, but she pulled a hand from her jeans pocket and gestured at the soulless structures. "Look at them! They fulfill every criterion for what is required for functional beauty: they perform their function, they are honest about the materials that are used, they don't pretend to be anything they are not. And what they *are* is ugly cages for people who have been robbed of their dreams, and whose greatest artistic aspiration in life is to write graffiti . . ." She jerked her head at some fat letters on the wall across the road. ". . . that looks exactly like everybody else's graffiti!"

"Yup."

"Beauty is not a necessary consequence of functionality and honesty."

"No..."

"Excrement is functional, and honest about the materials used. But it is not beautiful."

"True."

"Why are we here, Stone?"

"Dehan, can we save this discussion for tonight, in front of the fire with a glass of Bushmills?"

She frowned at me like I was crazy. "No, I mean why are we *here*, on Gleason Avenue, when I could be studying riverside premises? What do you hope to achieve with this?"

We had reached the playground and I stopped, looking up at the windows. "Remedios told us she was mad when she thought she'd seen a hooker standing on the corner, because this was not that kind of neighborhood, remember?"

She nodded. "So?"

"She said it was a nice neighborhood, in spite of your views on their soulless, functional architecture. So, at a little before nine on a Sunday night, we have a man assaulting a woman, on the street corner, in a nice neighborhood, and nobody sees or hears anything. That seems a little odd to me. Remedios told us she couldn't hear them because she had triple glazing in her windows, but she said the woman was shouting. So there must have been plenty of other people around here who did not have triple or even double glazing, who must have heard Celeste screaming at her attacker. Logical?"

Dehan was staring at me with narrowed eyes. I smiled at her and crossed the road to go and stand under the giant chestnut trees that skirted the playground. She followed me as far as the tree where Remedios had said Celeste had disappeared. There, I stood staring up at the buildings facing me across Gleason and Rosedale.

On the other side of Gleason was Remedios' block, and it was a fair bet her neighbors had not seen anything. She had told me nobody had discussed it with her, but I was pretty sure she had discussed it with just about everybody she'd met on the stairs and in the store at the time it had happened. I could always double-check later, but right now what I was interested in was the two redbrick blocks on the other side of Rosedale.

"Look," I said. "Those two uninspiring, functional buildings over there, on the corners, have a perfect, uninterrupted view of this corner. I make it four kitchen windows and a big living room bow window on that building." I pointed. "And a living room window and two bedrooms on *that* building. How old would you say those buildings are?"

She shrugged, still looking bemused. "I don't know. Seventy-five, eighty years old? Nineteen forties?"

I nodded. "Accurate." I pointed at the building with the bow window. "That one might be older. In any case, those windows look like the original sash windows to me. They are not shiny, plastic casement windows."

"Stone?"

"Yes?"

"I see where you're going. You think old, non-double-glazed windows, nice neighborhood, somebody washing up at nine p.m. or settling down to watch TV might have heard Celeste screaming."

"Yes."

"But Lenny already canvassed the area."

"Did he?"

I set off across the road. She watched me get halfway before she hurried to catch up.

"What are you suggesting, Stone?"

"Where does it say in the report that he canvassed the area for witnesses?"

I paused at the gate to the tall, late '30s box that overlooked the corner of the street. From here, I could see that the windows were indeed the original, wooden sash windows.

"It doesn't," she said, flatly. "But he spoke to Remedios, and it says there were no other witnesses. It would have been nothing short of a dereliction of duty to have the case go cold without canvassing the neighbors. Why would Lenny do that?"

"I don't know, Dehan. I don't even know if he did. It doesn't say anything about interviewing neighbors in the report." I pointed across the road toward Remedios' block. "Remedios Borja came forward on her own. Nobody knocked on her door."

I shrugged and pushed through the gate.

There were two blocks with six apartments per block. We struck gold after half an hour, when I knocked on the door of the apartment on the top floor, overlooking the corner of Gleason and Rosedale. Dehan was ringing on the bell across the landing, where she was getting no answer. The door I was knocking on was opened by a slim man in his midthirties wearing a V-necked, dark blue cashmere sweater with his white shirt collar on the outside. His jeans were carefully ironed, and his hair was carefully brushed. His eyes observed me, and Dehan over my shoulder, in turn, carefully.

"Yes?" He asked it as though there might be consequences.

I showed him my badge. "I'm Detective John Stone. That's my partner, Detective Carmen Dehan."

"Does *she* have a badge?"

I turned. Dehan showed him her badge.

He nodded once. "How can I help you, Detectives?"

A man's voice called from inside, "Who is it, Richard?"

"It's the police!"

"What do they want?"

He smiled at us without humor and shook his head. "If you'll give us a chance, I'll find out!"

"Forgive me for breathing, I'm sure!"

Dehan came and joined us. I said, "Two years ago, there was an incident down by the playground. We were wondering if you might have witnessed anything."

"My goodness, two years ago. I suppose we might have, but who remembers?"

I gave him a moment. When he didn't say any more, I asked,

"Do you think we could come in and ask you a few questions? It might jog your memory."

His body and his face said it was inconvenient, but he said, "Well, of course. You'll have to forgive us, Jack is cooking and we have friends coming for lunch . . ."

I nodded like I understood and reassured him, "It won't take more than a couple of minutes."

The door opened directly onto an open-plan living and dining area, with a large, modern kitchen separated by a wood-paneled bar. Jack, wearing a blue-and-white-striped butcher's apron and holding a pot and a wooden spoon, turned to look at us in astonishment as we came in. He was older than Richard by about ten years, and heavier by thirty pounds.

"Hello!" he said, as though that was a reprimand.

Richard gestured to us with both hands. "These are Detectives Stone and Dehan, and they are going to quickly ask us a few questions about an incident two years back. And we are going to help them." He turned to us and pointed to a suede sofa. "Please, sit down."

He sat in a black leather armchair and Jack approached from the kitchen, saying that he hoped the good karma he earned from helping us would prevent his sauce from burning.

When he had sat in the other chair, Dehan said, "Two years ago, 'round about this date, in November, there was an altercation outside, on the corner, opposite the grocery store. It would have been somewhere between eight thirty and ten o'clock, between . . ."

Jack was giving his head little shakes. He leaned back in his chair and crossed his right leg over his left, wagging his finger in a negative. "No, darling," he said. "It was later than eight thirty, and it was well before ten. I'll tell you, it was November sixth, at about nine o'clock on the button. Perhaps the whole thing lasted from five to nine until five past, if that."

Richard turned to him and voiced my own question: "How can you possibly be so sure and precise, Jack? You're showing off!"

He was still wagging his finger, but now he stopped and pointed it like a gun at Richard. "I'll tell you exactly why. That appalling woman, Monica Fraser..."

"Oh my goodness, you are absolutely right!"

Jack turned to me. "She wanted us to attend an event to rally support for a demonstration the following day, a Monday if you please, Mothers against Trump or some such idiotic nonsense. The event was at..."

Richard said, "Nine thirty! He is absolutely right—"

"Let me tell it, Richard. And she telephoned to us at a quarter to nine, begging us to go. Well, I told her, I am nobody's mother! Why would I go? Anyway, I fobbed her off and no sooner had I hung up than we heard this infernal racket outside. We both went to the window and there they were."

Dehan glanced at me. I made no effort to hide my "I told you so" face. She asked, "There who were, Mr....?"

"Kitzler, Jack Kitzler." He closed his eyes, still leaning back in his chair, and projected his hand forward, as though he was placing somebody on a stage. "The girl, dressed like a miserably unhappy Little Red Riding Hood. She is standing on the sidewalk, just a few paces from the chestnut tree. She has her hands in her pockets—the pockets of her red coat—and she is shouting. She is not shouting across the road, but diagonally..." He moved his outstretched arm to illustrate where she was shouting. "To a truck that was parked directly opposite our window."

I stood and went to the window. Dehan joined me. I said, "On Rosedale, to the left of the traffic lights."

"Exactly."

Richard had risen and was peering out with us. I asked, "Did you see what direction the truck came from?"

It was Richard who answered this time. "No, but I think we both had the impression it had just pulled over and stopped. It was facing left, south, so it had either come from further up Rosedale or it had turned in from Gleason."

I returned to the sofa. Dehan sat on the windowsill while

Richard sat on the arm of Jack's chair. Dehan asked them, "What happened?"

Jack said, "At first, I thought she was just a sad crazy, screaming at people that existed only in her poor, tortured mind. But then I saw there was a man climbing out of the truck, and then it became evident that she was screaming at him. He approached her, and at first, it seemed that he was speaking to her in an almost calming, reassuring way. Did you get that impression, Richard?"

Richard nodded. "Yes, I did. You couldn't hear him. He was talking quietly. Then I remember he took hold of her shoulders, and that seemed to set her off. She started screaming her head off."

He looked at Jack, who continued, "She backed away from him. He went after her. It was a little alarming. Then she turned and ran, and he ran too. They vanished in the shadows of that big chestnut tree, opposite the grocery store."

I said, "Why didn't you report it at the time?"

They both sighed simultaneously. Richard said, "Well, we did."

Jack closed his eyes and shook his head. "Don't be dishonest, Richard. We didn't."

"Well, we *did*!"

Jack wagged his finger. "No, no . . . you're being equivocal, Richard, and that is tantamount to dishonesty." He continued talking with his eyes closed. "We did not report it that night. We were conflicted that night and we discussed whether to telephone to the police, and we decided not to. The reason being . . ." Now he opened his eyes and spread his hands. "There had been no crime committed. How many couples, late at night in the Bronx, have rows on street corners at the weekend? Hundreds! Goodness *knows* the police in the Bronx have their hands full enough with all the violent crime that goes on. Our calling out a patrol car because of a lovers' tiff could cost somebody else their life. And that was the basis for our decision that night." He sighed deeply and Richard looked down at the floor. "As it emerged later, our perfectly logical decision turned out to be perfectly wrong."

Dehan was frowning. "So, when *did* you report it?"

Jack's expression became curious. "Well, surely it's in your report. We read in the paper that a girl had been found downriver at Soundview Park, wearing a big, red woolen jacket. We decided to call the precinct, but we saw a couple of uniformed officers and a detective talking to one of the neighbors across the way. She was pointing at the playground and the tree and we just *knew* what they were talking about. So when they had finished, we called over the detective and told him what we'd seen."

I grunted. "Can you remember his name?"

Jack sighed, shook his head. Richard got up and went to a dresser against the far wall. He opened a drawer and pulled out a fistful of business cards. "People give us these things, we keep them as though someday we might use them, but we never do. Still, this time . . . Aha!" He held it out toward us to see. "Detective Leonard Davis, Forty-Third Precinct."

I nodded. "Hang on to that, would you?" I sighed. "So you told Detective Davis everything that you have told us."

"And more," said Jack. "Partly because it was fresh in our memories, but also because we described the truck, which we have not done for you."

"I was coming to that. Can you describe the truck?"

He smiled. "Not in much detail, I'm afraid. You may have observed that Gleason has considerably better lighting than Rosedale, and what little there is down Rosedale at that point is obscured by the trees. What we were able to see was a white or cream four-by-four. I can't honestly be sure if it was a pickup or an SUV. Can you, Richard?"

Richard was putting the business cards away, sliding the drawer closed. He shook his head. "No. I remember, as you say, Jack, it was cream or white, might have been dirty, parked in the shadow of the trees. I want to say it had a closed back, like an

SUV, but I might be making that up. It could well have been a pickup, like a Ford pickup."

"Anything else? Did you see the driver return or drive away?"

"No, nothing after that. I think we watched a movie and that was it."

I stood, and Dehan stood with me. I said, "You have been very helpful indeed. You happen to know if any of your neighbors saw anything?"

Jack stood, shaking his head. "We talked to them, but nobody else saw anything, except that girl across the way."

They waved to us from the door as we went down the stairs, and Jack hurried away to save his sauce. Out in the drizzle again, I stared over at the corner.

"That right there, in that depressing light from the streetlamps, in November in the rain. That was where she spent the last few minutes of her life."

"Assuming she was killed there and not at the river." She looked up at me, squinting. "How did you *know*?"

I shook my head and gave a bland smile. "I didn't. It was possible, so I explored and got lucky."

She thumped my shoulder. "Good call. Now buy me some lunch and explain to me why it was possible."

SIX

We took a short drive to the Hugh J. Grant Circle. I parked on Metropolitan Avenue, and we pushed through the door into the dark, warm interior of the Step In. It wasn't long open, so it was quiet, with just a couple of guys sitting at the bar. I grabbed a table while Dehan went and ordered two beers and two burgers. She came to the table a couple of minutes later with the beers, put one in front of me, and sat.

She said, "A guy with a white or cream truck who works at one of the sites on the river between Starlight Park and Soundview. It doesn't exactly pinpoint our guy, but it's not the worst pool of suspects we ever had."

I made a noise of agreement and took a pull on my beer.

She pointed a finger at me. "But here's what's really on my mind: one, why the hell did Lenny not include these witnesses in his report? And two, what made you suspect that Lenny had come across a witness he didn't want to report?"

I looked around the dark bar at the high-gloss brass and dark wood, trying to organize my thoughts. I said, truthfully, "I didn't suspect it. I thought it was a possibility."

"Why?"

I sighed and spread my hands.

She rolled her eyes. "Okay, Sensei! What was it that made you think it was a possibility?"

"Several things. First, when we spoke to Remedios, she told us the guy appeared on foot. Now, as we saw later when we went to look at where she was washed up, it was a very difficult task to take the body to a place where he could dump it in the river. So one of two things happened: A, he abducted her and took her to the river, where he killed her; or B, he killed her on the spot and took the body away to dump it. Both of those scenarios require him to be driving a vehicle."

"Yeah . . . But Remedios said he arrived on foot."

"Actually, what she said was that suddenly he was there. If he had come down Gleason, walking, she would have seen him arrive. But if he came out of Rosedale, where Richard and Jack say they saw the truck, parked in the shadow of the trees, then it is possible she wouldn't see him till the last minute, stepping out of the shadows."

She nodded. "Uh-huh . . ."

"So at that point I decided . . ."

"Wait, at what point? Are we still talking to Remedios at her door?"

"Yes, of course."

"At that point you have already decided he had a truck parked down Rosedale. You have to be kidding."

I frowned. "Well, it was logical, Dehan. Either he abducted her or he killed her on the spot. If he had killed her on the spot, he wouldn't leave the body there and come back to collect it. So in both scenarios, he had to have a vehicle. The logical place was on Rosedale."

"Okay."

"Then I got to thinking about the neighborhood, which Remedios had described as 'nice.' And it struck me as odd that Lenny hadn't found any witnesses. Put that together with the fact that the phone records were missing, and I began to wonder if Lenny was trying to hide something. I didn't *suspect* . . ."

"It was just a possibility worth exploring."

"Precisely. So now we have a telephone number we can't trace because we have no phone records—and in any case, Lenny tells us it's a burner—and we have a truck which, had we not come to canvass the area ourselves, would also have gone undiscovered. A truck which was probably used to dispose of Celeste's body. Two years ago, it would have been a gold mine of DNA."

"Why would Lenny want to hide evidence like that?"

"Close the question and the answer will leap out at you."

"What would make Lenny conceal . . . okay . . ."

"Reynolds makes a big thing of the fact that he and Lenny were friends and grew up on the same street and they are members of the same Catholic church. Lenny plays it down, but he went out of his way to stress to me how much he hated giving the old man the news of Celeste's death: his oldest daughter diagnosed as schizophrenic, his wife died in childbirth, then the very child whose birth killed his wife was murdered and he, Lenny, had to tell him . . ."

A waitress arrived with our burgers and told us to enjoy them. I picked up one of the fries and put it in my mouth and asked Dehan, "Have you seen a white pickup recently?"

She frowned with the burger halfway to her mouth, dripping ketchup. "Yeah . . ."

"With tools in the back."

She nodded. "Yeah . . ." Her face cleared and she put down the burger. "Holy . . . Samuel."

"Samuel. When he got back from all his shopping."

Dehan's gaze became abstracted. "Celeste has reached that age. She has a crazy sister, a crazy dad, and a crazy brother. Plus God alone knows what dark feelings of guilt about having killed her mother. She hits puberty and her hormones turn her life into a living nightmare." She flopped back in her chair and looked at me, still holding her burger. "So she becomes that nightmare and starts making her dad and Samuel's lives nightmares too. It is a lot more than either of those two simple souls can cope with and the home environment soon becomes totally toxic. After two or three years of this, she and they are all fit to explode. Dad seeks refuge in his religion and his belief in family. Hell, it was probably the original cause for his angina and his high blood pressure. And Samuel is left with the whole burden of the family's deepening tragedy."

I smiled. "You should write those true crime stories, Dehan. I'm right there, living it."

I bit into my burger and wiped my mouth and fingers with a paper handkerchief.

She looked at me resentfully. "Shut up. The situation becomes intolerable when she starts sleeping around. She is, to coin a phrase, adding sin to insult. On that weekend, she comes in having spent practically two whole days and nights out. They confront her; she refuses to talk to them and storms up to her room. But then, not content with having spent Friday and Saturday night in sin, she now tells them she plans to spend Sunday night in sin too. She walks out. Samuel cannot take it. He calls her and tells her he is coming after her in the truck. She certainly doesn't want Samuel turning up at Chad's house and humiliating her, so she decides to confront him at the playground and tell him to leave her alone. Samuel turns up in his white pickup, parks on Rosedale, and the rest is history.

"Except that a week later, her body is washed up on the banks of Soundview Park. Lenny is called to the scene and recognizes Celeste. He talks to Sean and Samuel, learns about the fight, checks the phone records and talks to Richard and Jack, and puts the pieces together. This is going to be the final blow for Sean. The one member of his family he has left, whom he depends on entirely, is going to prison for the rest of his life for murdering his daughter. It will kill him. So, to protect his friend, he suppresses the evidence and lets the case go cold."

"Admirable," I said through a mouth full of burger. "So how do we go about proving any of this?"

She stared at me a moment, then took a big bite out of her burger and we both sat chewing and staring at each other.

"Fob a shtart . . ." she said, maneuvering the words around her food, "we need to find out where Samuel works. We also need to filter out all the businesses along the river that are impossible dumping sites for one reason or another: there is no riverbank at that spot, there is no access to the river, that kind of thing. Then we start cross-referencing people connected with Celeste with people connected with that list of businesses, see if anything pings."

"Good. We also find out how long Samuel has had that truck. If he only bought it last week, we have a problem."

"Find out what Chad drives."

I watched her lick ketchup from her fingers and nodded. "Yeah, there is something else too."

"Whamph?"

"Celeste's phone records."

"You said there was nothing we could do about that."

"I'm wondering. Lenny said he'd look at home. I'm kind of betting he won't find them. If he doesn't, what else can we do?"

She pointed at me like a gun, then wagged her finger up and down. "I was going to say. We should be checking her email. Where the hell is her computer? Eighteen-year-old kid with no computer?"

"Email. Exactly. Any longer messages will be on Facebook or her email. I'll talk to Reynolds today and see what happened to her computer."

She was watching me, squinting, and chewing her lip. "What do you plan to do about Lenny? His motives may not have been personal gain, but still, you can't let a murderer walk free just because it will upset his dad. Lenny has to be brought to account."

"I know. I agree. But I don't want to spook him just yet. If he's been concealing evidence and we spook him, we might lose any chance of ever recovering any of it."

We finished our beer and made our way back to Fteley

Avenue. As we were walking into the detectives' room, Lenny approached on rapid, short legs.

"Hey, Stone! How you doing, pal? Listen, you were right, I had the phone records at my house. I must have took the file home to study i—due diligence, right?" He laughed a nicotine laugh and slapped my arm. "And the damn page slipped out or whatever. I left it on your desk. How's it going? Doing any better than I did?"

Dehan was watching him with narrowed eyes and her hands in her back pockets. It made her look like a hawk about to pounce.

I shrugged. "It's a bit of a brick wall. I can see why it went cold."

"Right?"

"But, listen, you said 'page'?"

"Yuh." He nodded vigorously. "The phone records."

"Just one page?"

"Sure. How many pages you want?" He laughed again.

"Well, at least six months' worth, Lenny. How many days did you get?"

"One. What the hell! I was only interested in who called her that night!"

Dehan stepped over, her face screwed up like she'd just bitten a lemon. "You asked the phone company for the records on *one day*? What were they doing, charging by the hour?"

"Hey, take it easy, Wonder Woman! And can the attitude! What? You accusing me of not doing my job?"

People had started to turn and look. I said, "Nobody's accusing you of anything, Lenny. Relax. I was just hoping to go back over her calls leading up to that weekend. It's no problem. Thanks."

He scowled at Dehan and then at me. "Yeah," he said. "Now I know why you're both so damned popular! Accusing fellow officers ain't cool. Don't expect too much cooperation from me from now on. Screw you!"

Everyone who'd been watching turned away and got busy. Dehan gave me an eloquent look and we made our way to our desks. There was a slim manila folder on my laptop. I opened it and pulled out a single sheet of printed paper. I studied it a moment and saw the names of the people she had called, or who had called her, written in the margins. One number was listed simply as "burner."

I glanced at the top of the page and then tossed it over to Dehan. "It's a copy of a printed email document. Look at the top left corner. Those marks numbers he's tried to blank out. This is page two of one hundred and eighty. He got the whole six months up to the day she died."

She picked up the sheet, stared hard at it, and then stared at me. "How stupid is he? How stupid does he think we are?"

"They are good questions, and 'not very' has to be the answer to both of them."

"Huh?"

"That's not stupidity, it's panic."

She raised an eyebrow, but I ignored her.

I thought for a while. "Let's not focus too narrow just yet, Dehan. Let's continue with the plan we had, but perhaps we need to spread our net a little wider."

She sat forward and started typing. Absently, she said, "I have no idea what you're talking about."

I stood and went to look over Dehan's shoulder as she worked. I smiled. "You think you haven't," I said. "But you have."

"Yeah?" She looked up at me and grinned.

I winked at her. "Tell me if you get a hit, or what you find anyway. I'm going out to the car to talk to my pal at the DMV. And, Dehan?"

"What?"

"If you find something, try not to look triumphant."

She nodded. "I hear you, Sensei."

Out in my Jag, I slammed the door and sat thinking for a while. Finally, I called Mike, an acquaintance at the DMV who often helped me out. After greeting each other and reminding each other we had promised to grab a beer sometime, he asked, "What can I do for you, John?"

"Oh, it's just a couple of small things, Mike. They are a matter of public record, but you can find them in a matter of minutes and it would take me forever."

He laughed. "You could always use the computer!"

"If I did that, it would take me not hours, but days."

"Okay, shoot."

"I need to know what vehicles are registered to Samuel Reynolds." I gave him the address and hesitated.

He said, "That'll take five minutes. Anything else?" I was silent so long he eventually said, "John? You there?"

"Yeah, Mike, find out also what vehicles are registered to Leonard Davis, would you? Just email me the results to my personal email." I gave him Lenny's address, thanked him, promised we would get together soon, and hung up. Then I sat there five minutes, drumming my fingers on the wheel and thinking. Eventually I climbed out of the car and saw Dehan coming out of the station house door. She hunched her shoulders against the cold and the drizzle and loped across the road on long, slim legs. She looked up into my face. My phone pinged. I opened the email and read it.

I said, "Samuel Reynolds has owned his white Toyota pickup for the last six years."

"You're not going to believe this," she said, as though I hadn't spoken.

I said, "I think I might, though."

"After two years, the number is still assigned to a burner, Stone. It hasn't been used since that night, when it was used to call Celeste. But I nailed the location where the call was made from."

I smiled. "See? This is why I married you." She didn't laugh. Neither did I. I said, "It was made from here, at the station house, wasn't it?"

She didn't say anything, she just nodded. "How did you know?"

"Because Samuel called her from the landline at the house. So why would he call again, minutes later, from a burner? Also…" I showed her the email on my phone. "Lenny Davis has owned a cream Cherokee Jeep for the last four years."

SEVEN

She looked away and ran her fingers through her wet hair.

"Stone, this is starting to look like a lot more than concealing evidence to protect a friend."

"I know, but we shouldn't jump to conclusions yet. Lenny is a jerk, but he's also a good cop. One thing is protecting Sean from an escalating family tragedy, but Lenny as a killer? I find that hard to believe."

"The evidence is staring us in the face, Stone. Two blocks from where we're standing, he turns left onto Rosedale, and two minutes later, he parks at the playground." A cold breeze moved down Fteley Avenue and she fingered a strand of damp hair from her eyes.

I didn't answer straightaway, and I sighed. "It's circumstantial. He owns a white truck, so does Samuel, so do thousands of other New Yorkers. The call was made from the station house, but that doesn't mean that he made it."

"If not him, who?"

"That's not proof, Dehan. It makes Lenny a prime suspect, up there with Samuel, but it's not proof."

She frowned at me. "Well, what do you want to do?"

"We need to talk to the inspector . . ."

She nodded. "I agree."

"But before we do that, I want to go back to the Reynoldses' and see if we can locate Celeste's computer. There is no mention of it in Lenny's report. It has to be somewhere. Maybe she didn't have one, but that's unlikely. If she did and we find it, then we might strike gold with her emails."

She didn't look happy, but she nodded. "Okay."

We climbed back in the car and followed the route that Dehan had suggested. It was, like she'd said, fast and easy. Only, instead of going all the way up to the playground, we turned right for three blocks on Watson and then left into Beach Avenue. Dehan sighed as I pulled up outside the house, spread her hands, and shook her head, like she'd been having some long, internal dialogue with herself.

"I'm going around in circles. You're right, anyone could have made the call and got to either the Reynoldses' house or the playground in just a few minutes. But, like you yourself *also* said, Samuel *had already called her on the landline*. And Chad called her from *his* phone, so why would either of them then jump in a car, drive down to Story Avenue, call her on a burner, and drive up to the playground? It doesn't make any sense!"

"I agree, it doesn't make sense, Dehan. But we need to take baby steps here and not jump to conclusions. For a start, we don't know for a fact that it was Samuel who called her on the landline. We only know that somebody called her from the house." I shrugged. "Plucking a theory at random from thin air, maybe Helen called to warn her that Samuel was in a rage and had gone after her! Perhaps Samuel went to the station house to talk to Lenny, to ask him to intervene because he believed Chad was leading Celeste down the path of perdition. Lenny couldn't help, so Samuel called Celeste and said, 'Wait for me, we need to talk.'" We stared at each other for a long moment, then I went on. "I'm not saying that's what happened, I'm saying we need to be very careful that we are sure of each premise before we accept it as a fact. Right now, we don't know who used the burner."

She nodded. "Okay, yup. You're right. Let's go get that computer."

The slam of the doors sounded somehow damp in the gray afternoon light. Dehan followed me to the door of the ugly cube of a house and I rang the bell. It was Helen who opened it for us. She stood awhile, smiling, her eyes appearing to see things we could not. She was in her early thirties, blond, and could have been pretty but for the expression on her face that said, however far you searched, you would never find her.

"Hi, Helen." I smiled at her. "Is Samuel at home?"

"He's not here. He's gone."

"How about Sean? Can we see him?"

She frowned. "I took my meds. But that isn't always clear. Samuel is dealing with that."

Dehan said, "May we come in, please, Helen?"

She nodded. "Yeah, that should be okay. I just have to be careful not to let them start." She stood back and we stepped over the threshold. Dehan closed the door and Helen said, "Talking to me."

"May we go through to the living room and see your father now?"

"I was in my room. So far, that seems to be okay . . ." She nodded and made an almost placating gesture with her hands. "But I mustn't go out because they play tricks on me and I don't know how to get back. The stairs are okay, and so far my room is pretty solid."

I smiled at her again. "That's good news. Would you like us to take you up to your room?"

She nodded. "That's probably okay."

We climbed the stairs with her to a long, dark landing that led onto an equally long, but darker passage. At the end, the bathroom door stood open, and a dull, gray light, insufficient to make shadows or contrasts, showed another door, on our left, that also stood open onto a dark room. I pointed to the door.

"Is that your room?"

She nodded.

I asked, "Don't you want the lights on?"

She shook her head. "No, they told me the darkness keeps it all from cracking. The light has vibrations that make things crack. It's okay for other people. Samuel is strong, but Daddy is cracking. So for now, I'm playing it safe." She smiled. "Keeping things tight."

Two more doors stood closed, and at the far end, opposite the bathroom, a third. She pointed to the door next to hers. "Samuel is there in case they start making problems. I don't know how they get in, but Samuel can usually make them shut up. He says for now, the way forward is to take the meds, and pray to Our Father. I'm not sure, but I do what he says, for now. Play it safe is what I say."

I said, "And your daddy sleeps downstairs . . ."

"Until we can fix the cracks. We'll have to see how that goes. We're trying to find the right balance. He used to sleep in that room. But he's gone now."

She pointed to the room next to Samuel's. Which left the one at the end, opposite the bathroom, as Celeste's. Helen stared at that door for a while. When she spoke, her voice sounded empty. "Celeste took Mom away, and then she went away too. They get sucked through the cracks. We're trying to make sure Daddy doesn't get sucked out, but we'll have to see . . ." She crossed the landing toward the dark door, speaking over her shoulder. "I better get back. That's a lot of light for one day. Let's hope this rain keeps up. Bye."

And she closed the door.

I followed Dehan back down the stairs into the hall. She snapped on the light, but the overhead bulb, held under a green, plastic shade, only seemed to add to the gloom. She moved to the mahogany living room door and knocked. We heard some grunting and shuffling, then Reynolds' voice, shrouded with recent sleep.

"Who is it?"

"Detectives Dehan and Stone, Mr. Reynolds, may we speak to you briefly?"

There was silence, then some creaking of bedsprings, then, "Yes, I was sleeping, but come in."

We opened the door. The room was almost as dark as Helen's, except that gray light managed to creep in through the window that gave onto the backyard. Outside, shreds of wet washing dripped from a clothesline, and tall, scrubby blades of uncut grass quivered in the cold wind. Sean was up on one elbow.

"I was asleep," he said again. "Where's Samuel? He'll see you."

We sat without being invited: Dehan in the armchair where she'd sat before, I on the straight-backed chair by the window, where I could see his face better.

"It's actually you we would like to talk to, Mr. Reynolds. Just a couple of minor details." I smiled. "No need to trouble Samuel with them." I glanced at my watch. "Four o'clock. I imagine he's at work, right?"

He nodded. "More than likely."

"Where does he work?"

"He's self-employed. He's a welder, amongst other things. That boy can turn his hand to anything. Godsend to me: fix a washing machine, fix your car, even fix a leak in the roof."

"He's a fixer."

"He sure is that. What did you want to ask me?"

Dehan said, "Did Celeste have a computer?"

"'Course she did. She was never off the damned thing. When she wasn't on her damned phone, she was on her computer. I don't know what it is with kids these days, they always gotta be staring at some goddamn screen. It's either the damn phone, the damn computer, or the damn TV." He wagged a finger at Dehan. "I tell you this, them damn screens are gonna be the end of decent family life in this country. You mark my words. Separates the family. Breaks people up. Each one in her own room, glued to a damn screen."

I spoke almost without thinking. "Cracks . . ."

"What?"

"Cracks appearing," I said. "In families and society . . ."

He pointed at me. "That's exactly it. Family is the basis of society, and there are cracks appearing. I always said so. The Lord guide us, for we have gone astray."

"Mr. Reynolds, where would Celeste's computer be now? Did Lenny take it away?"

His eyes became abstracted and he stared into the gloom, as though he was seeing something that wasn't there. I had seen the same look on Helen's face a little earlier. "No," he said. "No, I don't believe he did."

Dehan asked him, "What happened to all Celeste's stuff? Where is it now?"

"Up in her room." He shook his head. "We haven't had the heart to go in and do anything. I know we should, but my angina and my blood pressure, anytime I think about . . ." His face crumpled and he started to cry. "I can't. I can't just kick her out like that, chuck her out with the trash. I can't do that . . ."

"Of course not, nobody would expect you to do that. You should treasure her memory."

He nodded at her, with his mouth open under wet cheeks. "Thank you."

"Sean," she went on, frowning. "Are you saying that Celeste's room is pretty much as it was that Sunday, when she walked out?"

He blew his nose and wiped his eyes. "Hasn't been touched."

"Lenny didn't go up there?"

"He said he didn't need to. 'No need to go upsetting you, old friend,' that's what he said."

I nodded a few times. "Well, Lenny is a good man, but I am afraid we are going to need to go up and have a look around, Mr. Reynolds. We need Celeste's computer."

"I understand. Just makes me cry every time I think . . . Don't break anything, or throw anything away, will you?"

"We wouldn't dream of it, Sean. And we won't take anything without your permission. But we do need her computer."

"Okay . . ."

We climbed the stairs again and found the door unlocked. I pulled some latex gloves from my pocket and saw that Dehan was doing the same. I pulled them on, pushed open the door, and switched on the light. The room was large, and tidier than I had expected. A window at the far end overlooked the street. The drapes were closed, and I went over and pulled them open. The bed was made, but under the duvet, the sheets were rumpled and not fresh. The pillows still had indentations, as of a head. There was a desk with very little on it. I looked at Dehan. "Call Dispatch, get them to send a forensic team out."

She frowned as she pulled out her cell. "Forensics? What are you expecting to find?"

"Something. I'm not sure what."

She made the call while I went through the desk and found nothing there. She had boxes below the desk. An exploration of them revealed stuff from when she was a kid. There was no laptop, no cable, no box a laptop once came in.

Dehan hung up. "They're on their way." She moved to a pine bookcase and started going through the books. "Mostly chick-lit," she said. "Women complain that they are stereotyped, then they read chick-lit and dress up as vaginas." I laughed. "Seriously, Stone. How many guys read guy-lit and dress up as penises?"

"Not many that I know of."

"Exactly. This looks like a diary." She took it over and leaned on the windowsill, started leafing through it. "It's from a few years back. Twenty thirteen, she's what? Fifteen?"

"Mm-hm."

I looked around. There were no posters on the walls. The books on the bookcase were, as Dehan had said, mainly chick-lit, but adolescent, as though she had bought them at the time of the diary. There was absolutely nothing in the room to suggest an eighteen-year-old Celeste had ever occupied it.

Dehan spoke again, while reading, "This is just page after page of complaint about Samuel, her sister, and her dad. She doesn't talk about any boys she likes, friends at school, bands . . . nada. Her whole damn life seems to revolve around her frustration with her family."

She snapped it closed, pulled an evidence bag from her pocket, and bagged the diary.

"Stone, how can Lenny believe that he can get away with this? A murder investigation where it is clear that the victim received a call from somebody she probably knew, using a burner, minutes before her death, and he neglects to search her room. What the hell is he playing at? The phone records, the witnesses . . . He could not possibly believe that he could get away with that."

"I know." I went and stood next to her, she looking into the room with her elbows on the windowsill, I looking out at the damp, gray road. "And the weirdest thing of all is that he is too good a cop not to realize it's just a matter of time."

Outside, the forensics van pulled up. I sighed as I watched them climb out. "The computer isn't here, Dehan. But I think I might know where it is."

We went down and opened the door. Bob was approaching across the sidewalk, dressed in plastic and grinning among his beard. Behind him was his team.

"Hey guys, how's married life?"

"Hell, but you should know that, Bob. You've been happily divorced for years."

He laughed like Santa and asked, "What's it about? What are we looking for?"

I hesitated a moment. "We are looking for fingerprints that do not belong to the family. If I'm right, you're going to find overwhelmingly Celeste's prints and very few others, maybe Samuel, her brother. But there may be one other, a man, and if you run him through the system, you'll get a hit. Let me know immediately, Bob. It's important.

"Also, check the bed for DNA. Again, if I'm right, you'll find Celeste's and a man's."

He frowned. "Okay."

"It could be a delicate matter. Go on up, room opposite the bathroom. I'll tell Mr. Reynolds you're here."

I found Dehan sitting on the hood of the Jag with her long legs stuck out in front of her. Dusk was gathering, and she watched me approach with frowning eyes. "You think Lenny was having an affair with Celeste?"

I stopped in my tracks and thought about my answer. Finally, I said, "Somebody was. If not Lenny, somebody."

EIGHT

It was a short drive down Gleason Avenue in the gathering gloom to Chad's place. He had the drapes closed, but warm light was filtering around the edges, touching the iron railings and the trash cans out front. He opened the door, closed his eyes, and sighed.

"You know? It is really hard for me to focus on my work when . . ."

I decided to save him time and distraction and cut across him. "This will only take a couple of minutes, Chad, and the sooner we get it over with, the sooner you can get back to your studies."

"Fine. Come in."

He made way for us. We didn't go through to the living room, we stayed in the hall. He spread his hands. "What?"

"After your row, you made it sound as though you and Celeste might be fixing things."

He shrugged. "If you want to put it that way."

"Did she keep stuff here?"

"Yeah, she'd been doing that for a while. I think she was trying to move in. I told her . . ."

I interrupted him. "So when she went home Sunday. She didn't take that stuff with her. She left it here."

His face went blank. He hadn't been expecting the question. "Yeah, I guess so."

"What did you do with that stuff?"

He frowned. "Well, after a few days, it was obvious she wasn't coming back and she wasn't answering my calls, so I boxed it up and stuck it in the basement."

I could feel a hot pellet in my gut. I asked him the million-dollar question. "Was her laptop among that stuff?"

He nodded. "Sure. She kept it here because she thought her freak of a brother was trying to read her mail."

"We're going to need to take that stuff away, Chad."

"Knock yourselves out. I'm going to assume you have either authority or permission, and if you haven't, I don't want to know about it." He pointed to a door in the wall under the stairs. "Key's in the door. It's a big box labeled 'Celeste.' You'll find it."

The basement had a bare, concrete floor, which was largely hidden by an accumulation of junk that had not quite descended to the status of trash. It covered the rear and the left-hand wall. There were a couple of sofas, a couple of chairs, a big dining table, and it was all buried under more crates and cartons than you could easily count. The crates and the cartons contained everything from books and magazines to old toys, ancient Nintendos, vinyl records, tennis rackets and baseball bats, plastic bags full of cassette tapes, and an infinite number of receipts for everything imaginable. There was also dust, a washing machine, a dryer, and an old fridge.

We made a plan of attack and worked methodically. The plan was to take everything that was on the left and rear of the room and put it on the front and left, item by item, until we found the carton with Celeste's name on it. We cleared a sofa and two chairs and moved two years' worth of receipts and invoices, essays, reports, and magazines from on top and underneath the dining table to the back of the room before we eventually found it.

It was not a carton. It was a semitransparent plastic IKEA storage crate with a blue lid, like a giant Tupperware box four feet long, three feet across, and eighteen inches deep. It was sealed with packing tape, and across one of the strips of tape, her name was written in indelible black ink. I lifted it and carried it to the table. There, I cut the tape with my Swiss Army knife and we removed the lid.

It was mainly clothes: jeans, blouses, shirts and T-shirts, a Columbia University sweatshirt, several pairs of panties and a couple of bras, socks, a pair of Timberland boots. There was a copy of the *Lord of the Rings*, and also a copy of Albert Camus' *The Outsider*. On the first page, there was a dedication to Celeste from Chad, dated two weeks before her death. I flipped through the pages and saw they were annotated in what seemed to be Chad's handwriting. I handed it to Dehan, removed a pair of Levi's from the crate, and found the laptop with its power cable and wireless mouse.

We stood staring at it for a moment, then Dehan dropped the book by Camus and picked up the *Lord of the Rings*. She leafed through the first pages. "There's no dedication on this one," she said.

I shook my head. "Looks like he was trying to educate her."

"There is more to Chad Norris than meets the eye. A touch of Professor Higgins."

She dropped the big tome back in the crate and I resealed it. "Let's get this back to the station and go through it." As we climbed the stairs back up to the hall, I sang, softly, "Oh, why can't a woman be more like a man?"

Dehan snorted ahead of me. "Actually, Stone, I was referring to the play, *Pygmalion*, by George Bernard Shaw, not the popular musical by Lerner and Loewe."

"Sure you were. That's because *you* are Eliza to *my* Professor Higgins."

"Jerk."

"See? *Quod erat demonstrandum*."

"Jerk."

When we reached the hall, I handed her the box and the keys

to the Jag. "Give me five minutes, will you?" She made a question out of a frown and I said softly, "Guys' stuff."

I opened the door for her and she went out to the car. I closed the door and went into the living room. He was sitting at the dining table, staring down at an open book. He spoke without looking up.

"What can I do for you, Detective? There is no need to come and say goodbye."

I leaned with my hands on the back of a chair, looking down at him. He sighed and looked up. I said, "Camus, *The Outsider*."

"What of it?"

"Were you trying to tell her who you were? Or were you highlighting what you both had in common?"

"I wouldn't read too much into that, Detective."

"Define too much."

He laughed. "Excellent! You should be a lawyer."

"Let's quit fencing, Chad. Your relationship with Celeste was a lot deeper—meant a lot more to you—than you have led us to believe. You can deny it as much as you like, but any jury in New York is going to see right through your denials. They've seen enough reality TV to recognize denial when they see it."

He held my eye a moment, then said, "A jury?"

"You want to tell me why a guy who's in love with a girl would lie about it?"

He made a face of derision and snorted. "Any number of reasons!"

"How about when that girl gets murdered one block from his house after he discovers she's been having an affair?"

He sighed and dropped his face into his hands. "I didn't kill her."

"I'm supposed to take your word for this?"

He dragged his hands down until they were in a praying position in front of his mouth.

I kept talking. "You lied to me before about your relationship and your feelings for her. That was a stupid thing to do, because it makes you look guilty. Give me one good reason I should believe you now."

He looked down at the book in front of him and closed it. "I can't. I acted without thinking. I had feelings for her. She was a pain in the ass, she was difficult, she was wild and much too emotional, sometimes she was overwhelming. But when she wasn't around . . ." He shrugged. ". . . I missed her. I guess I felt I needed her." He frowned at me, as though I'd said something he disagreed with. "She didn't get in the way of my studies. It actually helped me, having her around. And she was smart. We had conversations . . ." He smiled. "You can't do that with a lot of chicks. But she was getting restless. She had nothing to do. She wasn't academic. I was encouraging her to read. I'm not a fan of Camus. I never yet heard of an existentialist who invented a vaccine or a space probe. But she was into all that fancy foreign café society shit. So I bought her *The Outsider*."

"And you read it."

"I speed-read it so we could talk about it."

"You really cared about her."

"I've already admitted that, Detective."

"So when you found out about Rod . . ."

"It was tough. I'm not the jealous type, whatever you may think. We had a row, she promised she'd been stringing him along. What I told you about that was true."

"Except you said you hadn't called her, and you had."

He flopped back in his chair, eyes closed, then sagged forward and took a deep breath. "Yes, I had."

"What made you lie about that?"

"After Celeste disappeared, I decided I had to reinvent myself as a hardheaded son of a bitch. I try to cultivate that image. If you do that enough, eventually the image becomes real."

"What did you talk about when you called her?"

"I asked her where she was and if she was coming over. She said she was on her way."

"Did she say whether she had spoken to Rod?"

"No."

"Anybody else?"

He frowned, remembering. "Yeah . . . She said she'd had a big row with her brother and with her dad. That was why she hadn't come earlier. She'd been in her room. She needed to be alone or something. Then she'd walked out and her brother had called her, telling her to come home. Her dad was freaking out, having an angina attack or something."

"Did she say where she was?"

"On her way."

"You didn't go to meet her?"

"I was going to, but she said not to."

"What did you do when she didn't turn up?"

He shrugged. "I watched a movie, then went to bed. I assumed she'd gone to see Rod."

I frowned. "That didn't strike you as odd behavior?"

He laughed a nasty, harsh laugh. "No. That's women. They can change their feelings in a couple of seconds: 'Oh, I'm crazy in love with you, but oops! I don't really like the way you bend your legs when you sit and, and oh wow! Your friend has such big, brown, vulnerable eyes, now I'm in love with him.' That's women. Nothing they feel ever has any real depth or substance. It is never constant or real in any meaningful sense. You just have to live with it. After a couple of days, I boxed up her stuff and moved on."

I grunted. "Okay, Chad. Don't leave town."

"I don't plan to," he said, opening his book again. "I plan to prepare for my exams, if you'll let me."

Outside, a steady rain had started to come down. Through the windshield, I could see Dehan sitting behind the wheel. Rivers of silver light lay across the blacktop. I raised my collar, crossed the sidewalk, and climbed in the passenger seat. I closed the door and she smiled at me.

"So did you talk guys' stuff?"

"Yeah. He supports the Dodgers."

She turned the key and the engine roared. As she pulled away she said, "Anything else?"

"He confessed that his feelings for her were stronger and deeper than he'd led us to believe. That it was in fact she who was growing bored, not the other way around."

The windshield wipers squeaked and thudded.

"He admitted he spoke to her on the phone?"

"Yup. He called to see why she was taking so long. Quite a turnaround from his earlier statement. She said she was on her way, and that Samuel had called her saying the old man was having an attack of angina."

She turned left onto Gleason, past the post office. "He was using his illness as emotional blackmail: Daddy needs his family with him, especially his youngest daughter. She was always his baby girl. She has to come back to the fold. He sends Samuel to go get her . . . That's why she stopped to wait. Maybe she was planning to go back with him. Or, more likely, tell him to go take a hike . . ."

I interrupted. "Go back to the station, will you?"

She glanced at her watch. "Yeah?"

"Yeah. I was hoping we could catch the inspector before he goes home."

"Sure." She waited a bit. "Care to share?"

"Yeah . . . I don't know, Dehan. It's a feeling. Chad opened up, he seemed to be sincere, but when I asked him what stopped him from going out to look for Celeste when she didn't show up . . ." I shook my head. "It seems odd, doesn't it? They are making up after a bad row, she has come close to cheating on him, he has come close to breaking up with her, but they got through it and now they're fixing it . . ." I paused, visualizing it in my mind. "She's on her way . . . She tells him, 'I'm on my way,' but when she doesn't turn up, he doesn't go looking for her. He just assumes she's gone off with Rod. It doesn't gel. It's not congruent."

She joined the traffic on Watson, headed east. It was a wet blur of lights through spattered drops. The wipers squeaked and thudded and we crawled slowly toward Rosedale.

"You asked him?"

"Yeah, he said, women are like that. Their feelings change from one second to the next. Nothing they feel is constant or real in any meaningful sense."

She made a "maybe" face. "Wow, that's harsh, but he has a point. Not all women, but brother . . ."

"Carry on that way and you'll talk the thought police after us. I certainly don't believe he has a point. But, be that as it may, Dehan, it doesn't seem congruent to me. He accepted it too easily; after the fight and the makeup sex, and her spending most of Friday and the whole of Saturday there, when she is late returning, he calls her—note that he *does* call her—and then, at the last minute, when she is actually *on her way*, he gives up because of a stupid generalization: women are like that."

We turned onto Rosedale and stop-started our way under the Bruckner Expressway. The rain grew heavier.

"It is odd," she said, and then, "What are you suggesting, that he's altered that part of the story because he went to meet her and found her with this Rod character? They had a fight and he killed her?"

"It's a very tempting theory; unfortunately, it's not what the witnesses saw."

She was quiet for a while. We came out the south side of the bridge as the rain turned to a downpour. We turned right and crossed Soundview into Story and moved slowly toward the station house as the rain drummed on the roof and pelted the windshield. She said, suddenly, "Well, hold on there a minute, Stone. What *did* the witnesses actually see?"

I stared out at the deluge, aware that she was glancing at me for some kind of a reaction. When I didn't say anything, she went on.

"They saw Celeste, real mad, shouting at some guy who seems to have got out of a white truck. They saw them argue. They saw him grab her shoulders. They saw her turn and leave, and him go after her. After that, everything was hidden by the dark and by the giant chestnut tree. We don't know what happened after that point. As far as the actual killing is concerned, the witnesses saw nothing."

NINE

Dehan pulled in front of the door to the station. I grabbed the Tupperware box from the back seat and ran through the rain up the steps to the main entrance with Dehan just a few steps behind. At the foot of the stairs that go up to the second floor, we bumped into Lenny coming out of the detectives' room. He stopped and stared at me a moment, gave Dehan a hostile glance, and then said to me, "Look, uh, Stone, about earlier..."

"Don't sweat it, Lenny."

"No, I spoke out of turn. Just, you know, if it looks like somebody is questioning your integrity... You'd be the same, right?"

"Sure I would. No harm, no foul."

"That's big of you, man." He slapped my shoulder, then paused to look at the box. He grinned, but his eyes were curious. "What's that, your lunch box?"

Dehan's presence at my shoulder was intense. I wondered if she was going to say anything, but she just stood and stared at Lenny. I gave a small laugh, held his eye, and was deliberately misleading. I said, "We checked Celeste's room. These are some of her belongings. We found her computer."

His face hardened. "You found her computer in her room?"

"I figured you'd looked for it there," I said. "But it's always worth a second look."

"I went over the room with the old man. I'd swear there was no computer there."

I smiled at him for a moment, then said quietly, "No, we haven't found anything in her room yet. This was at her boyfriend's house, Lenny. She'd left it there."

His voice was wooden. "Oh. What else do you hope to find there?"

"What do you mean?"

"You said you haven't found anything . . . yet."

"Oh." I nodded once. "Traces of Rod. CS team should be on their way back to the lab by now."

". . . Rod . . ."

"Yeah, you don't know about Rod, Lenny. He only emerged in the last day. I have to go and talk to the inspector, but hang around and I'll put you up to speed, if you're curious."

He stared at me for a long moment, then shifted his stare to Dehan, then back to me. "Yeah," he said in the same wooden voice. "I'll do that. Catch you guys later."

He watched us start up the stairs, then pushed his way out into the rain. As we climbed, Dehan was staring at the steps like she was trying to read Chinese algebra. "Hang around and I'll put you up to speed? Remind me why we're going to see the inspector? Isn't it because we suspect the guy you just told to hang around and you'd put him up to speed . . . ? Have I missed something? Did I blink?"

I smiled sweetly at her. "Apparently you did."

I knocked on the inspector's door.

"Come!"

I pushed open the door and Dehan went in ahead of me. Deputy Inspector John Newman was standing by the window, putting on his coat. "Ah, Dehan and Stone, you just caught me. I was on my way home. My wife is making lasagna tonight, with fresh, homemade pasta, and I am charged with getting some wine on the way home. I must not be late. How can I help you? What a frightful night, isn't it?"

"We won't keep you, sir, but there are one or two points that have come up in the Celeste Reynolds investigation which suggest pretty strongly that the investigating officer at the time behaved, at the very least, inappropriately."

"Oh, Lord." He frowned and rested his backside on the edge of his desk. He pointed at the big Tupperware box I was holding with some difficulty. "What's this?"

Dehan said, "It's Celeste's laptop. We haven't examined it yet, sir. The reason we are here is that the original investigating officer on this case, Detective Leonard Davis, was a friend of the victim's family. The family are, to put it mildly, sir, dysfunctional. We have a number of possible suspects for the murder . . ."

He looked surprised. "Already?"

I sighed. "That is kind of our point, sir."

Dehan plowed on. "It looks as though Detective Davis may have suppressed evidence in order to protect his friend, Celeste's father . . ."

He frowned. "Protect him from what?"

"From the truth, sir, that his son might have killed his daughter."

"Good heavens! You have stirred up this much trouble in just twenty-four hours? I am not sure if you two are my greatest asset or my greatest liability! What makes you think this? Please, make it brief. I must get home."

I said, "The briefest look at the case immediately throws up the need to examine Celeste's phone records. I assumed that Detective Davis had requested those records back in the day, but they were not in the file. I asked him about them. At first he said he had no idea where they were, but then after I insisted, he said he would look at home. He came back next day, sir, with one page, saying that was all he'd requested. But it was a printout from an email that was over one hundred and eighty pages long. That's six months of records."

He sighed and looked at his shoes. "So he had requested six months of records, removed the records from evidence, and only showed you one page."

"Yes, sir. That page shows that in the short while before her death, she received calls from the landline at her home, her boyfriend's cell, and a burner cell. We have reason to believe that the burner belongs to somebody called, or using the name, Rod, and that she was having an affair with him."

"Can't you get another copy from the phone company?"

"That company is Verizon. They only hold records for a year, sir."

He sighed again. "And you think this Rod is Lenny, Detective Davis."

"That's putting it a little strong, sir, but the possibility exists. He neglected to follow up witnesses, he also neglected to question Celeste's boyfriend, failed to get this information regarding Rod, and he neglected to conduct a thorough search of Celeste's bedroom, telling her father that it wasn't necessary. I've had the crime scene team go over the room. There is a chance we may get fingerprints and DNA from her bed."

"Oh, Lord . . . This is a nightmare."

"Sir." I hesitated a moment. "I don't want to do anything about this just yet."

A flicker of hope in his eyes was rapidly replaced by a shadow of worry. "You don't? Why?"

"We don't know yet what his involvement is. It may have been a simple, misguided desire to protect Sean Reynolds from yet another family disaster, or it may have been something considerably more serious than that. I'd like to get the results from the lab and see what we can get from her emails before taking any action. It should shed more light on what Lenny's involvement was, and give us a better idea of how to proceed."

He thought about it for a while, still staring at the floor. "Does he suspect that you are, so to speak, onto him?"

It was Dehan who answered. "Yeah. He was pretty freaked out

at the fact that we had found her computer, and that we were taking in her bedding for DNA testing."

He studied her a moment before saying, "I can't put a tail on him without alerting the IAB. Plus it would cause a lot of resentment among the troops."

I smiled. "He'd spot it anyway, sir." I frowned and puffed out my cheeks. "I've known Lenny a long time, we're not friends, I don't particularly like him, but he's a good policeman. It's a difficult call to make, sir, and I might well be wrong, but I can't see Lenny being guilty of anything more serious than . . ." I spread my hands. "Extremely poor judgment. What I mean to say with that is—I seriously doubt he will do a runner. What is much more likely, I think, is that he will come and talk to you."

He nodded, like that made a lot of sense. Then he looked up at me and nodded again. "Yes, thank you, John. I hope you're right. Either way, it is hard to see a good outcome to this situation." He looked at Dehan, like she might have an answer. "A good professional with a lovely wife, two great kids, why would he get himself caught up in something so . . . *tawdry*?"

He stood, shaking his head. "Well, you two will be wanting to examine that laptop, and I must be getting home with the wine if I don't want to face a hearing of my own. Proceed as you see fit, but keep me posted."

He hurried on ahead of us, down the stairs, across the wet floor, and out into the wet night. We followed at a more forlorn pace, and when the inspector had disappeared, I said, "I think we've caused enough trouble here, Dehan. Let's go home and see what bombshells lie in Pandora's laptop."

And we too stepped out into the wet, November night.

———

WHILE I OPENED the wine and peeled and cut the potatoes to make fries, Dehan had a hot shower and came down in dry jeans and a sweatshirt, toweling her hair.

"I just hope to Christ she used an operating system prior to Windows 8."

I eyed her. "Why?"

"Windows 7 and earlier didn't use a sign-in page. Let's hope she used an email client too. Or we're going to have to hand this over to the techs." She plugged in the cable and sat down, thinking aloud: "Twenty sixteen. Windows 10 was launched that year, there was never a Windows 9, did you know that? And 8 was really unpopular. It was crap. Millions of people actually downgraded back to Windows 7 because they hated 8 and 10 that much. So I guess we have an even chance that she might . . ."

The familiar Windows jingle sounded and she smiled. "It's Windows 7, and *dude*! She has Thunderbird."

"So her emails are downloaded automatically to the laptop?"

"Yup."

I put the fries in the hot oil, dried my hands, and pulled up a chair beside her. She opened the Thunderbird app and, after a moment, the emails were listed. There were a couple of thousand of them, all but the last five or six marked as read. The last few were dated between the fourth and ninth of November. I flopped back in my chair. Dehan voiced my thoughts.

"Where do we begin? At five minutes per email, that's going to be a hundred and sixty-seven hours. If we worked twelve hours a day nonstop it would take us . . . two weeks."

I looked at her a moment then laughed. "We don't need to do that. Take ten emails, identify the names that are not relevant. Put the ones that are not relevant into a folder. Keep going until you find a name that raises a flag. Then focus on that name."

She was nodding vigorously before I'd finished, saying, "Yeahyeahyeah! You're right."

"Also," I said, and stood. "Before you do anything else, search for Rod, see if it brings up an email address."

"Yeah, I know, I was going to do that!"

"Sure you were."

"Go away and let me work."

While she searched for any reference to Rod in Celeste's emails, and while the fries fried, I made an avocado salad with artichoke hearts, diced tomato, and a simple dressing of olive oil and Maldon sea salt. By the time I got to putting the griddle on to heat, I heard her sigh.

"Okay," she said, "here they are." I heard the printer whir and clunk and start disgorging pages. She stood and leaned on the breakfast bar. "There are only six," she said. "But they are pretty intense." She went and collected the emails from the printer and brought them over. "They only cover a week, and they are from six months before she died."

While I read, she poured two glasses of wine and placed one next to me.

The first was from Lenny, and it was a reply to a long email from her complaining about how her father and Samuel controlled and pressured her, how they were constantly complaining to her and trying to force her to go to church and live in a way that made no sense to her. She was desperate to get out of the house and away from them. She had, she said, nobody to talk to. She ended up by apologizing for writing to him and saying that she had enjoyed chatting to him outside the church, and it was nice that he had visited her dad a couple of times recently. She hoped he would come again.

His reply was brief but friendly, rather than friendly but brief.

Hey, Celeste! Nice surprise to hear from you. How's the family? Yeah, I enjoyed our chat too. Don't often get to talk to somebody who 'gets it'. So many sheep, right? I'd definitely like to drop in and see your dad (and you!) if I'm in the area. Hope to catch Samuel in too, though I'm not always sure when I can get a free half hour.

THE NEXT EMAIL from her told him exactly when Samuel was out and how her dad liked to sleep for a couple of hours after lunch. Then it suggested that that might be a good time because they could talk freely in her room without worrying about Samuel and her dad.

The next email was not from Lenny's email account. It was from rod_wheeler.

Hi Babe, listen, I don't want to go all cloak and dagger on you but I can't receive emails like that at my personal email account. Most people just would not understand and I am not exaggerating if I tell you it could cost me my job and my marriage. But I gotta tell you, it put a big damn smile on my face. I can't think of a way I'd rather spend my lunch hour...

It went on in that vein. The next were obviously after their encounter and it was obvious that they had had sex. She was besotted, if not with him, with the idea that he could somehow set her free, talking about eloping together to California to live in the desert. And he was half out of his mind with the fact that at his age, he had somehow seduced an attractive eighteen-year-old girl. Instead of telling her that things had got out of hand and he had to break it off, he nurtured her dream, knowing as he must that he would never leave his wife and kids, and he could never make it come true. It made grim and depressing reading.

The last one said that they had to stop using email. It was too risky, and he wanted her to delete all the emails she had sent him, and the ones she had received from him too. He was going to buy a burner and they could call each other and use WhatsApp to communicate. It would be better, he said. In her reply she promised to do that, and promised also to send him some "special" photographs.

I put them down and looked up at Dehan.

She shook her head. "Why didn't she delete the emails?"

"For the same reason he never got rid of the phone. They are a memento, a trophy even."

"I guess. So they spent the next six months having an affair. His DNA will almost certainly be on the sheets. He is ruined. His life is finished. Even if he doesn't go to prison, he has lost everything."

I nodded.

She went on, "And he has gone right to the top of our list of suspects."

I chewed my lip at her for a while, then went to throw the bison steaks onto the griddle, which was at risk of catching fire. They sizzled noisily and I turned back to Dehan and sipped my wine. "You're thinking that he found out about Chad and killed her."

"It's about the oldest and most reliable motive known to man, and woman."

"Lenny and Chad, and Celeste in the middle, two-timing both of them."

"Which one is the killer?"

"Take your pick."

She thought about it for a moment while I turned the steaks. Then, she said, "My money is on Lenny. Lenny killed Celeste."

TEN

I had called Frank, the ME, and Bob, the head of the CSI team that had examined Celeste's room. They had both gone home but agreed to see us first thing in the morning. First thing in the morning, for them, was six a.m. So at five fifty a.m. the next day, we were pulling off Seminole Avenue in the darkest hour before the dawn. We found a parking space, killed the engine, and made our way to Frank's office: a small pool of light in an empty building in semidarkness. Bob was there with him. They were drinking coffee out of paper cups. They both looked up as we pushed into the lab.

Frank made the expressionless face that for him was a grin and said, "When newlyweds start getting up before six in the morning, that is a bad sign."

Dehan grabbed a chair and said, "This from a man who gets all his social interaction from corpses."

Frank raised an eyebrow, and I sat, so we were all gathered around his desk.

"They often have more to say than the living, believe me," he said. "But my point is, what has you two up and about at this hour of the morning? Usually it's just weirdos like me and Robert."

She pulled Celeste's laptop from her bag and handed it to Bob. As she did it, I said, "For now, this has to stay very quiet between you, us, and Deputy Inspector John Newman. It is not urgent the way other cases might be urgent. This started out as a cold case, the murder of Celeste Reynolds, but it has pretty quickly become clear that the case did not go cold through lack of evidence..."

Bob was frowning hard. "What do you mean?"

"It went cold because the detective investigating it was suppressing evidence: he hid evidence, failed to look for witnesses, and didn't follow up on obvious leads. In a sense, that was fortunate for us, because as a result, he failed to find her laptop. He looked for it in her room but didn't find it, because it was boxed up in her boyfriend's basement, and he never interviewed her boyfriend."

Bob looked squeamish. "I dread to ask what's on it."

"At first glance, it looks like a brief exchange of love letters. The evidence is pretty strong that the emails come from the investigating detective, but we need proof from your tech guys that the original email address is his, and that the new email address is also his." I paused and held Bob's eye. "Obviously, Bob, if we have a detective who has murdered an eighteen-year-old girl he was having an affair with, that is something that has to have the highest priority. We don't know if he is doing the same thing to some other girl right now."

He sighed, nodded, drained his paper cup, and picked up the computer. "I'm on it, I'll give it to the nerds right away."

"And, Bob? The sheets you took from her room? The semen on them might be his. It also has to take priority. I need to get you a sample of his DNA somehow..."

He shook his head. "Lenny Davis is in the system. You'd be surprised how many are. They are profiled for purposes of elimination, and the profile stays in the database. You're probably there yourself."

He got up and left the office, taking the laptop with him. Frank said, "You are determined to make my life a misery."

"It can't be helped, Frank. If Lenny had sex with Celeste in her bedroom, it puts him very firmly in the frame..."

"You don't need to tell me, John. It is not just physical evidence of a motive for murder, it's a lot more than that."

Dehan frowned. "What do you mean?"

He leaned back in his chair, so that the back of his head was touching the sickly green wall. "How old is he? A bit older than you, Stone. Late forties, early fifties? He's married, he has kids, a long-standing career with the NYPD, and a spotless record. He has everything to lose.

"You tell me he is an old friend of the family of the victim, and the family have a record of tragedies: a schizophrenic daughter, the wife died in childbirth, and the victim herself turned out to be wild." He shook his head like he was looking at something that defied belief. "If he had met an *adult* woman and had an affair out of town, at a hotel, on the mature, adult understanding that it was going to go no further than a one-night stand, you *might* be able to accuse him of nothing more serious than poor judgment and bad taste." He shrugged. "If the department got to hear about it, they might even look the other way, having privately cautioned and reprimanded him.

"But with an eighteen-year-old girl, in her own home, with the risk of a member of her family walking in on them at any moment..."

Dehan was nodding that she understood. "I see what you're driving at. It's beyond reckless. But it's worse than that, the father is ill and confined to bed most of the time, so he was in the house, and her sister would have been just down the hall, in her room."

He spread his hands. "That is not just poor judgment and bad taste, that is a reckless disregard for consequences, not only to himself, but to the girl and her family. A man in that frame of mind should not be walking around with a gun."

I sighed. "Frank, is there anything you can tell me about the body? Anything that might help to identify where she was dropped in the river, anything about the killer..."

He sat forward and the jointed mechanism in his chair clunked loudly. He folded his forearms on the desk. "I won't say I was ahead of you, John, but I remembered the case. It struck me as odd at the time."

"What struck you as odd?"

"She had been strangled. She had a lot of bruising around her neck and there were marks on her esophagus that were clearly thumbmarks. There was no water in her lungs, so it was clear that she had been strangled and dumped in the water postmortem."

"Yeah, we read that in the report."

He ignored me and went on. "She had been in the water for about a week. Now, the eccrine glands in the skin's surfaces on your fingers and palms secrete water that contains soluble solids. So prints deposited by *only* eccrine secretions get dissolved when the print is submersed in water. But it is possible for prints to survive in water or exposure to the elements if a non-water-soluble contaminant was present on the fingers, or if it was already present on the surface which has been touched."

"What are you driving at, Frank? In layman's terms."

"Well, for example, sebaceous glands in the skin secrete an oil called sebum into the hair follicles to lubricate the skin and hair. Then, also, women have a tendency to smother their skin in all kinds of oils, from coconut to aloe vera and beyond. All of these might—I stress *might*—survive a period of submersion in water, especially if it was very cold. So if skin covered in sebum, or aloe vera or coconut oil, for example, were pressed very firmly, the resulting print..."

Dehan's eyebrows had shot up. "Seriously?"

He frowned and nodded. "The FBI Laboratory's Latent Fingerprint Section, the Knoxville Police Department, and the University of Tennessee did a lot of research in the nineties developing a workable method for getting identifiable prints from human skin, even after prolonged exposure to the elements. What they eventually came up with was the glue fuming chamber. It has a built-in heat source and a small electric fan. You put glue into a small aluminum pan in the chamber and the glue fumes are gently blown out onto the prints for ten to fifteen seconds. After that, powder is applied, and often as not, you can lift a print."

I frowned hard. "Are you telling me that you lifted prints from Celeste's neck?"

He shook his head. "No, I'm not telling you that. We didn't, but listen . . ."

"You're losing me."

"I proposed using the glue fuming method to Lenny. I grant you it was a borderline case, she *had* been in the river for a week, but it was worth a try. We might have got something. The thumbs had been pressed very forcefully into her throat, and that would have increased or even caused oil secretion."

Dehan said, "But he said no . . . ?"

"He said it was a waste of taxpayers' money. After that much time in the river, he thought there was no chance of getting a print. He might well have been right, but I thought it was worth a try." He gave a laugh. "Especially as the family were friends of his. Usually what I get is pains in the ass like you two, hassling me to do more and go faster. I don't often get a detective telling me not to bother with a test."

I shook my head. "Son of a gun. It's a shame you didn't do it anyway. He doesn't dictate . . ."

"Oh, I did! I did! I'm not going to be dictated to by the likes of him. I did the tests. He was *partially* right. We got a few partials that were not really usable—not in court, anyway, though they *might* have been helpful in an investigation. He never came back to me, the case went cold, so I filed them away and that was it."

"So you have partials of Celeste's killer's thumbs?"

"I have *largely unusable* partials of Celeste's killer's thumbs. They might be suggestive, but they would not be conclusive or probative of guilt."

Dehan snorted. "It's a damn sight more than we had last night."

He shrugged. "I wouldn't be so sure. Personally, what struck me as most significant was the detective's refusal to have the test done."

I nodded. "That could be very significant. Frank, can you run a comparison of the partials you got with Lenny's prints? See how close they actually are?"

"Of course." He glared at me. "I *have* other work which also involves murder, people who are important to other people and killers who might strike again! But I will try and get it done today."

"You're the best, Frank."

"Now, both of you, get out and let me get back to work. The dead are calling to me. I must go to them . . ."

Outside, the eastern horizon was turning a smoky blue-gray and the air was shifting from night to grainy twilight. The traffic was desultory and had a sleepy quality to it, as though the occasional car, with its hazy headlamps, was driving out of a dream toward the waking hours.

Dehan opened the passenger door, but instead of climbing in, she leaned her forearms on the roof and looked up at the plane trees across the road, where the dawn chorus was starting its noisy chatter.

"What do we do now, Sensei?"

"We go to the station, we pick up some coffee and croissants on the way, we make a list of all the businesses that back onto the river from Starlight Park to where Celeste was found, and we start phoning them, one by one, asking for their lists of employees for November 2016."

She shifted her eyes from the trees to stare at me.

"Holy . . ."

"It's a Chinese puzzle, Dehan. Nothing quite answers everything."

"That's why you asked me who my money was on. You were already thinking about that."

I sighed and leaned my arms on my side of the roof. "The fact is it could just as easily be Lenny or Chad, though Lenny has worked much harder at incriminating himself. But whichever one you pick, you are still faced with the original questions: How the hell did they get her into the river, and why did they dump her upstream?"

She raised her hands and rubbed her face with her palms. "Why . . . *how* . . . would Lenny have access to one of those lots, warehouses, or factories?"

"The same question applies to Chad. Which is why we need to work systematically through those premises." I thumped the top of the car with my index finger. "That question, pretty much the first question we asked, Dehan, is key to this investigation." I paused, watching a pink-and-orange haze touch the horizon behind her. "I know Lenny has put himself in the frame, and I'm not saying he didn't do it, he may well have. But there is more to it than that."

She made a doubtful face. "An accomplice?"

I shrugged. "Let's go find out."

We spent the morning compiling a list of all the companies that had premises on the banks of the Bronx between Starlight Park and the northernmost point of Soundview Park on the river. By nine a.m., Dehan had drawn a detailed map showing each one of them, its location, trade, and telephone number. She got hold of a whiteboard and pinned the map to it, and we started working systematically through them all. It was a mile-long stretch on the east side of the river, and almost a mile and a quarter on the west bank, a total of eighty-five outfits, from small one-man shows, partnerships, and limited companies to corporations and state-owned enterprises, like parks. Many of the addresses on the Bronx River Avenue above Colgate were private homes that backed onto the railway lines before the river, adding two more layers of complication to the puzzle: Did he know somebody with a house up there who helped him dispose of the body? And if so, how did they get the body over the tracks and through the fences before dumping it in the river?

At nine, Dehan went down to the deli on the corner to get more croissants and coffee, a practice which never failed to raise hoots of derision from fellow detectives stuffing their faces with the more traditional donuts. While she was gone, I started calling.

It was slow, tedious work that yielded very few results. Mostly you got a vaguely amused voice saying something along the lines of, "A poisonnel rawstah? 2016? Sure, listen, I'll tell yah what I'm gonna do for yah, pal. Soon as Frank gets in, I'm gonna tell him to prioritize dat for yah and send it right over, FedEx." And you hung up knowing full damn well that nobody called Frank worked there.

Other times you got a more efficient-sounding secretary, but she'd tell you pretty much the same thing: they'd have to dig out the records, scan them, and email them over. They'd do that just as soon as they could.

Dehan returned. Mo hitched his pants over his belly and wheezed a laugh in what he thought was a French accent. "Oooh, ear she come, wiz zee qua-sonts and zee ca-fay!"

She put down the coffee and dropped the croissants, squinting at him like she was trying to see him through a dense mist. "What the hell is wrong with you, Mo? You sound like you have my neighbor's dachshund stuck up your ass. Didn't your mommy tell you to stop playing that game with small dogs?"

There were general snorts and sniggers around the room. Mo gaped. She ignored them all and sat. "How's it going?"

"Dreadful would be accurate, if restrained."

We kept going for another two and a half hours, securing lots of promises to send us over the list of employees for November 2016 as soon as they possibly could.

At ten minutes before noon, Bob called.

"Hey, John, listen, I finished the tests, and I'm afraid I have some bad news for you."

"Whatever it was, it wasn't going to be good news, Bob. Go ahead."

"Right. Look, the sheets showed positive for semen as well as other fluids. The semen was from just a single donor . . . It's Lenny's DNA, John. He had sex with the girl in her bed, in her house."

I was quiet for a moment, then I said, "I understand, Bob. Thanks."

"Frank will contact you later about the other thing. I'll send over my report with his."

"Yeah, that's great. Thanks."

I hung up. Dehan was watching me. I said, "Let's go talk to the inspector."

ELEVEN

The rain had started again in earnest. Outside the inspector's window, the world was a gray, misty place, and from the lintel, cold, silver pearls of water gathered and dripped onto the sill below. An occasional wind shook them from time to time and dispersed them, dragging the rain back and forth in the background, among the black shades of naked trees.

Dehan sat on the black vinyl, imitation leather sofa beneath that window, and I sat in the chair opposite him at his desk. Deputy Inspector John Newman looked at me unhappily and said, "What, precisely, have we got, and what do we know for a fact?"

I looked at Dehan. Her gaze shifted to the ceiling and she began to recite:

"We know, as of ten minutes ago, that Detective Leonard Davis had sexual intercourse with Celeste Reynolds at some time not too long prior to her death." She looked at the inspector and spread her hands. "The sheets on her bed were not pristine, but they were not dirty either. We know that he had been conducting a sexual affair with her for about six months prior to her death. We know that he registered a special email address to communicate with her, and that address contained the name 'Rod.'" She closed her eyes a moment. "Rod underscore wheeler at yadda yadda dot com. We know that after exchanging only a few messages, he told her it was too risky and asked her to delete their messages. He told her that he was going to buy a burner, so that they could communicate by WhatsApp. All of that we know as hard fact."

I gave him a moment to assimilate that and what it meant, then said, "We also know that when Detective Davis took on the investigation of Celeste's death, he concealed evidence, and that he did not employ due diligence in acquiring evidence. He requested six months of phone records from Verizon, her service provider—the six months during which he was having an affair with Celeste—removed them from the case file, and held them at home. We know also that though he was contacted by witnesses on the corner of Rosedale Avenue and Gleason, who saw Celeste in an altercation with a man who had arrived in a white truck, he did not include their testimony in the file. We also know that he did not interview Celeste's boyfriend, nor did he have a team conduct a thorough search of her room, though that would have been a logical step to take. In short, he deliberately allowed the case to go cold."

The chief had been nodding while I was talking, making an occasional note. Now he said, "What about his relationship with Reynolds?"

Dehan answered. "He tends to play it down. They knew each other as kids, attended the same Catholic church, right opposite Reynolds' house, but besides that, he says they are just acquaintances. To hear Reynolds tell it, they were a lot closer, and he was often at their house. That's borne out, sir, by the exchange of emails, where she refers to a visit from him."

He thought for a long time, staring at the floor over by Dehan's feet. Eventually, he took a deep breath and said, "None of this actually points to him as a murderer. There is strong circumstantial and forensic evidence that he was trying to conceal an affair. There is a strong possibility that that affair provided the motive for murder. But any decent defense attorney is going to have a field day destroying the case as it stands, and quite rightly so. This boy Chad has just as much motive, and from what you've told me, he is a young man with a very violent temper. There actually is, in point of fact, a reasonable doubt as to both of their guilt. You need to bring me something that nails either Lenny or Chad to the murder."

I said, "We may have that later today, sir. When Celeste's body was taken into the morgue, Frank managed to get a partial thumbprint from her throat. I have asked him to run a comparison with Lenny's thumbprint. We don't know at this stage how useful it will be."

He was thoughtful for a while again, then said, "It may be enough to make him confess. Bring him in. Let him believe the thumbprint is better than it actually is. See if he breaks. Either way, he's finished as a cop. Go find him. What a disgrace, to himself, his family, and the department. If you have to charge him, charge him with concealing evidence and the obstruction of justice for now."

We went down the stairs. Dehan went into the detectives' room, and I went to the front desk. Maria, the desk sergeant, was there.

"What do you want, handsome? That Carmen not treating you right?"

"Yeah, I need some sweet consolation from you, Maria. Oh, no, wait, it was something else. Yeah, you seen Lenny Davis?"

She frowned. "No, I saw him yesterday. He was goin' out when you was comin' in. But I ain't seen him today."

"Call me on my phone if he comes in, will you?"

"Can I call you on your phone if he doesn't?"

"No."

I met Dehan coming out of the detectives' room. "Nobody's seen him since yesterday. I asked Pete, his partner. He said he hasn't seen him since yesterday. He's called him a few times, but his phone is switched off. He said he wasn't feeling so good last night. I didn't want to push."

I nodded. "Let's go to his house."

We pulled our coats over our heads and ran through the downpour to the Jag. We clambered in and slammed the doors. I backed out, then headed at a snail's pace, with my lights on, down Story Avenue to Soundview, where I turned right.

Lenny's house was in Castle Hill, on the Avenue. It should have been a five-minute drive, but it took all of fifteen with the heavy traffic and the rain, and we finally pulled up outside his house at one p.m. His white Jeep was in the driveway, alongside a gray Toyota. I parked across the drive, so he couldn't leave, and then we climbed out and made a run for the front door.

His was one of a row of ugly, redbrick monoliths set in concrete front and back yards behind a white steel railing. The windows didn't invite you in so much as scowl at you from forbidding walls. Dehan leaned on the bell, and after a moment, the door was yanked open by a woman in her early forties with blond hair, a tragic mouth, and weeping eyes that first showed hope, and then despair.

"Oh, my God!" she said. "Are you from the precinct? Are you here about Lenny?"

Dehan said, "Can we come in? It's raining . . ." and squeezed past the woman. She stood back and I pushed in too.

She was staring up into my face with her hands half reaching for my lapels. I said, "Are you Lenny's wife? What's happened?"

She shook her head in rapid jerks. "I don't know! I thought you knew! I don't know what's happened to him." Now she grabbed my lapel and pulled herself toward me, staring up into my face with half-crazy eyes and smudged mascara. "His car is here! His phone is switched off. Pete called me asking where he was. I came home. There's nothing, just the note."

"What note, Mrs. Davis?"

"On his computer."

"Show me the note, and tell us, step by step, everything that happened since last night."

Her whole body was trembling. "You don't know then? You don't know where he is?"

I shook my head and spoke quietly. "No, but we are going to find him. Where is the note? Show it to me."

Dehan stepped up, put her arms around her, and the woman collapsed against Dehan's shoulder, sobbing convulsively.

We were in a small, carpeted hallway with white skirting boards and white walls. A door gave onto a small living room that was unremarkable. I leaned in and looked around for a PC but didn't find one.

A narrow staircase with white banisters climbed to an upper floor, and beyond Dehan and Mrs. Davis, I could see a door to a kitchen with mock parquet flooring. I squeezed past them and went to the kitchen. The door to the backyard was open, and the rain was making a loud, thundering roar on the concrete, spattering water onto the floor. I closed the door and looked around: a large fridge covered in notes and magnets, a calendar, an open dishwasher beside a washing machine, a draining rack with a cup, a small plate, a large plate, and a butter knife, a steak knife, and a fork. A pine table occupied the center of the floor, with four matching pine chairs. On it there was a laptop, closed. On top of the laptop there was a note.

I sat, pulled on my latex gloves, and picked up the note.

BABY, I am so sorry, I don't know where to start.

I have done something very, very stupid, and I have caused so many problems for you and for the kids, just through my own selfishness and vanity. If I could go back into the past and change what I have done I would. If there were anything on Earth I could do to change my mistakes, please believe me baby, I would. The last thing I ever wanted in this life was to cause harm or unhappiness to you and our beautiful girls.

I can't explain to you what has happened, or what I have done. There just isn't time. I have to go away. Please believe me, I would not do this if I did not have to. But I have no choice. It has to be this way.

Kiss the girls for me one last time, because I will probably never see any of you again. I love you hunny. Please believe that I always have and I always will.

Lenny

I BAGGED it and returned to the hall. Dehan and Mrs. Davis had moved into the living room and were sitting on a white leather sofa. I sat in a matching chair with my back to the window. The double glazing blocked out the sound of the rain, but somewhere I could hear the splatter of water falling from guttering onto concrete.

She had stopped convulsing, and her breathing, though shaky, had come under control. Dehan was stroking her back.

I said, "Mrs. Davis, have you any idea what this note is about?"

She was shaking her head before I had finished the question. "I thought you would know, when you turned up . . ."

"How was Lenny when he got home last night?"

She frowned and blinked a lot. "He was kind of, hyper." She turned to face Dehan as though she might understand what she meant. "A bit too boisterous, a bit too noisy, joking a bit too much."

"Was that unusual?"

Her face said she wasn't sure. "He got like that sometimes, especially in the last two or three years. It depended on the case he was on. If it was difficult, or involved long hours or surveillance, sometimes he would come home a bit hyper like that. But last night was a bit over the top."

"Did anything happen?"

"No, not then. Nothing special. We had dinner, we watched

some TV. Then, about eleven thirty, me and the girls went up. He said he had to do a little work on the computer and he'd be right up."

She stopped. Her bottom lip curled in and she started to cry again, speaking in a strange, twisted voice. "But I came down to get a glass of water. He didn't hear me, and I saw, on the screen, he was booking a plane ticket! A ticket to Mexico! Where is he *going*? Why is he *doing* this? What's *happening*?"

"Did you get any of the details of the flight, Mrs. Davis?"

"I think it said the flight was Delta, at fifteen twenty. That's three twenty, right?"

I stood and walked into the hall, dialing the inspector.

"John! What's happening?"

I spoke quietly, walking down to the kitchen. "He's gone AWOL. He's booked on a Delta flight to Mexico at three twenty. You need to alert the airports. Find out which airports have flights to Mexico at three twenty. Let me know and we'll head out to intercept him."

"Okay, stand by."

I went back to the living room. Mrs. Davis was talking to Dehan.

"He said it was part of an undercover operation, something to do with a drug bust, a joint operation between vice and homicide. He said the ticket wasn't for him. It seemed very odd to me, but you know, he never really wanted me to get involved with his work. He always said that home was his haven from all that. That's why . . ." She stared up at me. "It seemed so odd that he would be doing that at home. He never brought his work home."

"Has he packed any clothes?"

She nodded silently. "And his passport is gone. I haven't checked our account yet. What has he done?"

I sighed and said truthfully, "We don't know yet, Mrs. Davis. That's what we are trying to find out."

She turned to Dehan. "He got up with me this morning, which he has never done. He's always up very early. And he kissed me very tenderly when he saw me off at the door. I felt then it was like he was saying goodbye. Is he going to come back?"

Dehan squeezed her hand. "Let's just take it one step at a time. We are as surprised as you are, Mrs. Davis."

My phone rang. It was the inspector. "John, it's John here. We have a Delta flight out of JFK, at three twenty exactly. I have alerted security, though it's a bit late. If you get moving, you should have time to get there before it takes off."

I glanced out the window at the rain. I said, "Yeah, okay. We're on our way." I turned to face her. "Mrs. Davis, we are going to try to catch up with your husband before he boards the plane. We will let you know as soon as we know something. Meantime, have you got anybody who can come and be with you?"

She nodded. "I'll call my sister. Please bring him back to us."

Dehan gave her a hug and said, "We'll do our best. I promise."

The rain had eased from a monsoon to a steady downpour. We clambered into the Jaguar and I fired her up. As we pulled out onto the road, I smiled. Dehan said, "You're smiling. That is inappropriate right now."

I glanced at her. "It always amuses me," I said. "You are such a badass with such a bad attitude, but underneath, you're just a big, soppy blancmange."

She didn't answer. She just stared out at the rain as we moved north and then south toward the Hutchinson River bridge, but I thought I saw her smile.

TWELVE

The massive hall was packed with what looked like thousands of people. There was a hum of voices that echoed overhead almost like a cathedral. Behind me, the doors hissed open to the sound of the downpour, then closed, leaving only the smell and the shiver of the damp. Everywhere there were wet coats, closed, dripping umbrellas, plastic macs, red, blue, yellow, and transparent, milling, swilling, jostling, pushing, pulling, and carrying luggage of every shape and size.

I said to Dehan, "You find the Delta check-in desks. See if he's in the line or if he's checked in. I'm going to Departures. See if he's there or if he's gone through."

"K!"

She moved off through the crowd and I half ran, pushing through the seething, wet bodies toward Departures, scanning the crowds as I went. I knew the inspector had contacted airport security, but that was no guarantee that Lenny would be seen, recognized, or stopped. It takes time to set up something like that and make everybody aware of a particular face and name—a face and name that gets added to a hundred other faces and names to be on the lookout for. It would be enough for him to be wearing a hat, or glasses, for him to go through unnoticed.

I approached the long, curling line of bodies that was snaking its way through security into the departure lounge. There must have been two or three hundred of them, shuffling one by one through passport control and moving on toward the scanners.

I ducked under the tape and started making my way toward the passport control desks. A big, burly guy from Airport Security started moving toward me. I showed him my badge and he frowned. "Anything I can help with?"

I shook my head. "Not right now. I need to talk to the CBP officers."

I kept moving as I spoke, scanning the lines moving past each desk. And then, three desks down, the fifth man in the line made me look twice. It wasn't him; he had a moustache, a tweed cap, and heavy glasses. But something in the way he was moving: he was too tense, looking too fixedly ahead, the rise and fall of his chest was just a little too rapid. I pushed through the next line, making toward him, mentally removing the cap, the glasses, and the moustache. He must have seen me coming, he couldn't have missed me, I was fifteen feet away and closing, but he just stared hard at the floor ahead. I shouted, "Lenny!" I raised my badge over my head, pushed through the next line, and shouted again, "*Lenny!*"

Everyone was staring except him. The guys on the passport desks were looking over. The security guard was coming up behind me, talking on his radio. I pushed through the next line and he was just six feet away and I knew it was him. He turned to face me, removed the phony glasses, and as he did it, he pulled his piece from his holster and pointed it at me. His hand was steady and his voice was calm.

"Don't come any closer, Stone."

At first, nobody reacted. Then a woman saw the gun and screamed. It only takes one to seed panic. Next thing, everybody was shouting and screaming and running, but Lenny had collared the young man in front of him and had him in an armlock, with his automatic at the back of his blond head. The guy's eyes were wide with terror. His skin was sickly pale. The CBP officers were on their feet with their weapons trained on Lenny, as was the guy who had been following me.

I put my hands up. I still had my badge in my left. I spoke loudly so the security guards and passport control could hear me. "*NYPD! This man is also a police officer. He is wanted for questioning. Hold your fire.*"

Lenny shook his head. "I'm not coming with you, Stone. I'm walking out of here with this hostage."

The hostage made an inarticulate noise.

I said, "Come on, Lenny! You're a cop. You know how it works. There are only two ways this can end. You leave here with me, or you leave in a body bag. Let the man go. Put your gun down. Let me cuff you and take you back to your family."

He had started backing up toward the exit doors. He was nodding. "Sure! Sure! Back to my family. Like that is ever going to happen! You think I don't know what's waiting for me?"

There was the tramp of running boots. Armed cops were approaching from both directions with handguns and automatic rifles. Lenny shouted:

"*Back off! Back off! I don't want to see a single armed cop! I don't want to see a Home Guard! I don't want to see any security personnel! I don't want to see a single damned gun in this damned airport! Or this man gets it in the head! Understood?*"

There was a muffled scream from the hostage. The radios were crackling, and somewhere I heard somebody shout, "Who the hell is in charge here? Get the head of security down here, for Christ's sake!" I ignored them and kept pace with Lenny as he backed slowly toward the exit.

"Lenny, I just came from your house. Your wife is out of her mind with worry."

He pointed the gun at me. "You! Come closer. Come right up close. Keep pace with me. We're going out of here." His face suddenly flushed, and he screamed at the airport cops. "*I'm gonna* count to three! If on three I see one damned uniform, I'm putting this cop down! Now back up!"

Behind me, I heard a voice snap, "Fall back!"

I walked toward him as he had instructed me. With my hands up, at a steady, slow pace, talking quietly all the while. "What are your kids going to think, Lenny? You think they'll see this on the news?"

"*One!*"

"Is this how you want them to remember you?"

"*Two!*"

"You want them to be ashamed of you for the rest of their lives?"

"*Three!*"

I braced myself. I knew he would do it. I saw the muzzle of the gun point at my chest. Then there was a roar, like the roar of a lion, only it was a woman's voice bellowing, "*Back up! Now! On the double! Fall back! Who is in charge here?*"

I smiled and thanked whatever gods choose cops' partners for giving me Dehan. I saw Lenny swallow and we continued to back toward the exit. "You stay close, Stone, and if you try anything, I swear to God I will kill this man and I'll kill you too. You know I'll do it . . ."

We were twelve feet from the automatic doors. Outside, in the rain, I could see anti-terrorist troops in fatigues taking up positions. I wondered if Dehan was liaising with the head of airport security yet. I kept talking. "It's not too late, Lenny. You're in trouble. You're in pretty big trouble. But if you stop now, it's not too late. Your wife really loves you. Your kids love you. You don't need to lose all that."

He was shaking his head. "Shut up, Stone. You want to pin Celeste's murder on me, and that ain't gonna happen. I ain't taking the fall for that."

"You got it wrong, Lenny. We just need to talk to you, find out what happened."

He glanced over his shoulder and saw the troops. Cop cars

were arriving with their lights flashing, reflecting red and blue off the wet sidewalks and the asphalt. Uniforms were running, cordoning off the area.

"Call your bitch of a wife over here."

"No."

"This schmuck gets it!"

I saw the man's eyes go wide with terror. I stared Lenny in the eyes. "It's a line I won't cross. Shoot him, and before he hits the floor, you'll be dead. Shoot me if you want. I'm not calling Dehan over here."

His tongue flicked over his dry lips. "Tell her to call off these troops out here. I want a car, with the key in the ignition, and the engine running, full gas tank. You're coming with me."

"Okay, we can do that, just let this man go."

"Uh-uh, tell her, then I let him go."

I turned my back on him. Dehan was fifteen or twenty paces away, watching me. Another fifteen paces behind her was an army of uniformed cops in dark blue with body armor, and a similar number of troops in battle dress. I called to her.

"Call off the guys outside. We need a car, full gas tank, key in the ignition and engine running. I'm going as hostage. He's letting this guy go."

I turned and took a step toward him. I was maybe five feet away now. I could see sweat on his face. He had the gun pressed to the back of the man's head again. I said, "Okay, Lenny. I did what you said. Now let the man go."

"Uh-uh." He shook his head again. "I want you in cuffs, and I wanna see all those troops moved. The minute I let this guy go, they'll put a bullet through my skull."

"Not if you put your weapon down. You made a big mistake doing this, Lenny. Now you need to come back from the edge and we can work something out. Just lay down the weapon, and let the man go."

"Take a hike, Stone." He looked over his shoulder, out at the cops and the troops ranging around the exit. They were beginning to move back.

I inched forward. "You promised to let him go, Lenny. If you don't let him go, there will be no more concessions. They won't trust you. Let him go."

"Where's the car? When I have the car, I'll let him go."

"Have you thought this through, Lenny? For crying out loud, you're a cop! How many hostage situations have you seen where the hostage taker gets away? It doesn't happen. You know that."

He screamed suddenly, "*Shut up! I said shut up!*"

"Okay, I'll shut up, but I wish you'd think of your kids. You want them to see you get shot on TV?"

"*Shut up!*"

He thrust the gun at me. It was what I had been hoping he would do. I had closed the distance and I was slightly more than three feet away, so the gun was right in my face. It was all or nothing, right then.

I stepped forward with my left foot, taking myself out of his line of fire. Simultaneously I slammed my left hand hard down on his wrist and seized the barrel of the gun hard in my right, levering up as I did so. There was a loud report and a shot went off, up into the vault above. I tore the gun from his hand, I heard his hostage scream, and his legs started kicking. I knew as long as Lenny had hold of this guy I couldn't point a gun at him. So I heaved my two hundred and twenty pounds at them both, unbalancing them and making them both stagger backward. At the last second, as they were falling, I grabbed the hostage by the scruff of his neck and heaved him back toward me. The whole thing took no more than a couple of seconds. But as I pulled the man back, he clutched at my arm with frantic fingers, screaming hysterically as he did it. I hurled him away, trying to free my arm. The barrel of the gun caught in his jacket and his flailing arms knocked it out of my hands. I shoved him again, and as he fell back, his foot kicked the pistol away from me.

Lenny was sprawled on his back. I made for him, but he was

already scrambling to his feet, reaching for the weapon. I pulled mine from my holster. Behind me, I could hear boots running. I knew Dehan was coming up fast. I shouted, "*Stay back! He is armed! Stay back!*"

He fired two shots wildly and ran for the sliding doors. I shot at his legs as he ran, but I was off-balance and he was moving fast. I missed. Then I ran too. Outside it was still raining hard. He was drenched in seconds, but he was fit, light on his feet and fast. I went after him, shouting for him to stop, but I was hampered by my coat, which was heavy and wet. He was getting away from me, and up ahead I could see where the cops had made a barrier with their cruisers. The lights were flashing red and blue, and the officers were using the roofs and hoods to steady their aim. I shouted at them, waving my arms, "*Hold your fire! Hold your fire!*" And then, "*Lenny, for God's sake, they're going to shoot you!*"

Next thing, he had veered sharply left and was running for the edge of the road, where it was a sheer drop down to the next level, forty or fifty feet below. I bellowed at him to stop. He fired wildly at me again and I dropped to the road for cover. Then he was running again and I was going after him. I saw that several of the cops had broken from their barricade and were sprinting toward us.

I clambered to my feet again and went after him. I saw him step over the barrier. I screamed at him to stop. Then he jumped.

My stomach lurched and I went cold inside. The rain was lashing my face. I wiped my eyes with my hands to clear my vision as I went to the ledge where he had jumped. I could feel the water squelching my shoes and running down the back of my neck. I peered over, expecting to see his broken body on the wet asphalt below. Instead, I saw the roof of a covered walkway that stretched across the parking lot, and Lenny running unsteadily, slipping and sliding toward the far end. I turned and bellowed at the approaching cops. "*Seal the exits to the parking lot! He's in the parking lot! Seal the damned exits!*"

They turned and began scrambling back toward their vehicles, hollering instructions to each other. I stepped over the barrier and heard, dimly, Dehan's voice calling to me. I didn't wait to hear what she was saying. I jumped and landed in a slipping, sprawling mess on the steel roof. It hurt. I got unsteadily to my feet and ran, trying to ignore the pain, sliding and falling as I went. He was fifty or sixty yards ahead of me and not making much better progress than I was. The rain was coming down hard, kicking up a mist off the blacktop and getting in my eyes. Visibility was poor, and I was trying to keep my eye on him as well as run as fast as I dared.

Then I saw his arms go up in the air suddenly and he vanished. I accelerated my pace, thinking maybe he had been shot. I slipped and staggered and fell several times, cutting my hand on the wet steel. And as I approached the spot where he had been, I realized there was a drop of about six feet, to a lower level. I jumped down, then lowered myself to the ground and looked around. There was no sign of him. All I could see was an ocean of wet cars, and in the distance the flashing lights of the patrol cars approaching to seal off the exits. On foot, there was nothing to stop him gaining access to any of the other parking lots, roads, or even the freeway. I swore violently under my breath. Then up ahead, twenty or thirty yards away, through the cold sheets of gray rain, I saw the headlamps come on. And the big Dodge RAM accelerated straight at me.

THIRTEEN

The tires spun and screamed on the wet asphalt. Then they gripped, and the headlamps glowed and swelled through the mist of rain, heading straight at me. One second of indecision and paralysis is enough to get you killed several times over. One second was how long I stood, staring at the iron beast that was bearing down on me.

I leapt aside when it was just ten feet away. At the same instant, he spun the wheel, aiming to point the nose of the truck toward the gardens that separated the parking lot from the Van Wyck Expressway. The tires screeched but couldn't get a grip, and his fishtail turned into a spin. The back end caught me on one of the turns and slammed me against a parked VW. The Dodge wound up on the far side of the covered walkway, facing the wrong way, and I wound up on my back, croaking for breath that I couldn't get, staring up at the bellying, gray clouds with rain in my eyes and needles of pain shafting through my lungs.

The spasm eased. I managed to drag in air. I heard a powerful engine rev and struggled to lift my head and look. The Dodge RAM was forty feet away. Its headlamps made rivers of light among the spray. I looked behind me and realized that I was lying between the Dodge and the gardens that separated the lot from the expressway. Far off, I could hear sirens through the rain. The Dodge revved, the tires screamed, and the truck hurtled toward me. I struggled to one elbow, but my back went into spasm again and pain tore through my lungs. In my head, a voice told me to prepare for death.

Even as I thought it, I saw a shadow, like a ghost, placing itself between me and the truck: a tall silhouette, legs straddled. There was a sound like fireworks cracking. The headlamps loomed around the snaking form. Brakes screeched, the truck careened out of control. I felt its massive form slide past, just feet away, and then there was the shattering noise of steel smashing and tearing into steel, glass shattering, and car alarms crying out across the flooded, gray, concrete lot.

And Dehan was kneeling over me. "Are you okay? Tell me you're okay."

"Help me get up."

She hooked her arm under mine and I struggled to my feet. "I'm okay. Check Lenny. Is he alive?"

Her face loomed large in front of me. "Stone! Focus! Look at me!"

I scrunched up my eyes, wiped water from them, and blinked. She was hazy. "What?"

"Are you okay? Check! Don't just say yes. *Are you okay?*"

I scowled. "*Yes!* Go check on Lenny!"

"Stay there!"

She ran toward the mangled wreckage where the careening Dodge had plowed into three parked cars. I staggered after her, feeling unsteady on my feet, but managing to breathe a little easier. I could see the red-and-blue flashing lights of patrol cars speeding toward us from the far end of the lot. I could hear another approaching from behind. Dehan, drenched through, with her long hair shining black, wrenched open the driver's door on the truck and reached in. I leaned against the side and watched her. It was hard to tell her expression, but she wasn't happy, and she wasn't talking.

Two patrol cars skidded to a halt a few yards away and officers began to spill out. She strode toward them, holding out her badge. I heard her shout, "NYPD! We need an ambulance and some paramedics—*fast*!"

She conferred with a sergeant, giving instructions, then signaled to an officer to come with her. Between them, they helped me to the back of one of the patrol cars. A dull, pervasive pain was building throughout my body. She sat next to me and looked into my eyes for a long moment. "You are some piece of work, John Stone."

"You're not so bad yourself, standing in front of a charging Dodge RAM." I pulled out my phone and dialed. "I'm calling the inspector. We need jurisdiction on this. Is Lenny alive?"

While it rang, she said, "Just about. He took two rounds in the chest and one in the face."

"You only fired four times. Remind me never to get you mad —Sir? Stone here . . ." She touched my leg, climbed out, and, hunching her shoulders, loped away to where I could see an ambulance pulling up beside the crashed Dodge.

"John! What news?"

"We had an incident at the airport, sir. He pulled a gun, Airport Security were involved . . ."

"Did they shoot him?"

"No, not exactly. He ran, I gave chase, Detective Dehan was close behind . . ."

"Is she okay?"

"Yes, thank you, sir, so am I," I added with a touch of irony. "He tried to run me down in a stolen truck, but Detective Dehan shot him. He is still alive, but it doesn't look good."

"I see." He was quiet for a moment, then said, "She's something, isn't she?"

"She is. Sir, we need jurisdiction on this case. You'll need to contact Airport Security and make sure they understand it's our case."

"Yes, of course. Then I want you both back here as soon as possible for a debriefing. Can we say the case is closed?"

I closed my eyes and thought about it for a moment while my body ached. "I'm not sure yet, sir. There are a few factors that need to be looked at, and I am slightly concussed at the moment from being side-slammed by a Dodge RAM. Give me a while to think it through, would you?"

"Naturally, get yourself seen by a doctor, then my office. Good work, Stone. Both of you, outstanding."

"Thank you, sir."

I hung up and sat for a while, looking through the spattered windshield as they lowered Lenny out of the cab, put him on a gurney, and ran him, ducking through the rain, to the back of the ambulance. There they lifted him in and slammed the doors. Dehan spoke to the driver. Then the ambulance took off, wailing into the gray, wet afternoon. After that, she returned to the car with the sergeant, wiping her face on the back of her sleeve. They climbed in and slammed the doors. The sergeant was big and black and had the kind of smile that told you we could all get along fine, as long as you behaved. He half turned in his seat and gave me a look that was curious.

"You okay there? I heard you got fishtailed."

"It was more like being hit by a small moon, but I'm okay."

"Your friend in the Dodge was critical. They had to get him to hospital in a hurry, but we have a medic here. You want me to take you to see her?"

"No, thanks, Sergeant. I'd as soon get on. We still have a lot to do. You understand we have jurisdiction in this case?"

"I just heard that from the chief. There ain't no terrorist angle and no drug trafficking involved, so, far as I'm concerned, I'm happy for you to take it off our hands."

"Nothing like that. Can you drop us at my car?"

"You ain't gonna drive. I ain't askin'. You just ain't gonna drive."

I smiled. "No, my partner gets to drive today. I am just going to lie back and moan."

DEHAN DROVE BACK the way we'd come, but we made a detour via Morris Park to have a hot shower and change into dry clothes. We finally made it to the deputy inspector's office a couple of hours later, at shortly after four p.m., as the sun was preparing to set behind the heavy cloud cover, turning what should have been late afternoon into premature night. The rain had not eased, coming in relentless off the Atlantic, but a wind had picked up, and as we sat around the inspector's office after the debriefing, drinking coffee out of china cups, squalls spattered at the black glass, trickling liquid diamonds down the panes.

He, the inspector, gazed at the black glass for a while, listening to the cold weather outside, and said, suddenly, "No shade, no shine, no butterflies, no bees, no fruits, no flowers, no leaves, no birds—November!" He gave a satisfied smile and a gentle snort. "Thomas Hood. But at least," he added, sipping his coffee, "you have some good news, though I very nearly lost two of my best officers in the enterprise."

Dehan, sitting once again on the sofa beneath the window, gave her head a slight sideways twitch and looked unsure. "I have to say, sir, for my money, Lenny is our man. He's the guy. But I don't think Stone is convinced yet."

I sighed. "There are some things I am not clear about. I'd like to talk to him, if he pulls through."

The inspector frowned and set his cup down carefully on the desk. "His behavior, John, was the behavior of a guilty man."

I nodded. "Because he was, and is, a guilty man. I am just not clear exactly what he is guilty of."

He frowned and blinked a few times. "Well, clearly, we know that he was guilty of having an affair with Celeste Reynolds. But that, though reprehensible, is not illegal—not criminally so, anyway. She was of age, and they were both consenting adults."

"That's true."

"So, though it might explain his lies, the secret email account, and his secret telephone, it does *not* explain his attempt to flee the country, his pulling a gun on officers of the law, or, I might add, his attempt to run you down."

I studied him and drew breath. He seemed to have a slight aura. I looked over at Dehan and saw that she had one also. Either they were both becoming enlightened beings, or I had slight double vision resulting from concussion. I decided to go with the latter theory, because I also felt too tired to explain what to me appeared extremely obvious, but to them didn't seem to be clear at all. Instead, I said, "Well, let's see if he pulls through."

Dehan said, "I just spoke to the hospital. He's in surgery. His left lung is badly damaged and he lost a lot of blood . . ." She stopped talking, and I saw the corner of her mouth twitch and her eyes flooded. She took a deep breath and went on. "They won't know till tomorrow midday what kind of shape he's in."

The inspector gave her a moment to take a couple of deep breaths, then spoke quietly and kindly.

"Carmen, I know today has been very traumatic. Taking a life is always traumatic, we all know that, but when it's a fellow officer, it is especially so. However, he might pull through, and I want you to know that your actions today, in capturing a suspect and, more especially, in saving your partner's life, were nothing short of exemplary. You didn't take a fellow officer's life, you risked your own to *save* a fellow officer's life. You must remind yourself of that."

She managed a smile. "Thank you, sir."

"I can see that you are both exhausted, so I am ordering you to go home and rest. Order in, watch a movie, sleep. And sleep late tomorrow. To help you both do that, especially you, John, let me sum up briefly for you:

"Lenny, who had known Reynolds since he was a boy, and

had stayed in touch through the church they both attended, made the mistake of allowing himself to fall into a sexual affair with Celeste, Reynolds' daughter. No doubt at the time, he thought it was a harmless adventure. However, as so often happens in these cases, with men of that age, he found himself becoming infatuated. She was a deeply unhappy girl in a deeply dysfunctional family, and his own paternal, protective instincts got the better of him and led him away from the path of righteousness.

"She, as is perfectly natural in a girl of her age, fell in love with Chad, a boy who, though we may find him disagreeable, to her was the answer to all her prayers. But she did not know how to tell Lenny. So she strung them both along, avoiding the inevitable confrontation as long as she could. In the end, the inevitable happened, and Chad discovered her infidelity. He demanded she break it off, and that was what she tried to do, on the Sunday afternoon. But that evening, after her big row at home, as she was on her way to Chad's house, Lenny phoned, from this very station house, and asked to see her. She decided, as you yourself said, John, to see him and get it all over with, there in the street, rather than letting him meet Chad. But tragically, when she tried to break it off, his passion got the better of him, and he killed her. The witnesses saw him and his white truck right there, at the scene of the murder.

"When he discovered that you had her computer, and that you would find his emails, he knew he was lost, he panicked, and he ran. I'm afraid, John, that it could not be clearer. And I am confident that tomorrow morning, when you have rested and your brain has slowed down, you too will see it that way."

I made a one-shouldered shrug. "The witnesses all described a large man. Lenny was medium at best."

Dehan sighed. "From an upper floor, Stone, at night, in November, in the drizzle and half-concealed by the giant chestnut tree. Also, Celeste was pretty small. A man assaulting her in those conditions could well appear large."

I spread my hands. "You're right. I need a large whiskey and a deep sleep. Let's see how things look in the morning."

The inspector gave a big, satisfied smile that made him look oddly like Santa Claus after attending a health spa on a Caribbean holiday. "That's the spirit!" he said comfortably. "Take a couple of days' rest, you both richly deserve it."

We went carefully down the stairs. Dehan was saying, "Ordering in sounds like a good plan, Stone. You know what I fancy? I fancy a curry..."

I gave her a narrow-eyed smile and nodded like that was a nice idea.

She went on, "You probably just want a hot bath and a large whiskey, huh, big guy?"

All my back, my arms, and my legs were beginning to seize up. I walked like the Mummy toward the exit and said, "I hate baths. But the large whiskey sounds good."

We stepped out and she opened the umbrella she had thought to bring with her. She linked her arm in mine and we started across the road toward the Jag. The rain pattered loudly on the taut, black cloth. "You don't buy it, Stone, I know. But you have to let go, not be obstinate, and accept that for once you are not right. You are only half right."

"Okay."

She opened the passenger door and I climbed in with difficulty. She got in behind the wheel, stared at me awhile, and finally said, "Okay, what is it that's eating you?"

I shrugged. "What's been eating me from the start. How and why did he dispose of the body the way he did? Whichever way you look at it, it doesn't make a damned bit of sense. He just would not have done that." I shook my head. "He didn't kill her, Dehan. He is not the guy."

FOURTEEN

She backed out of the lot and turned left onto Story Avenue. Her face was rigid. The wipers set up a steady squeak and thud as the streetlamps washed the cab by turns with amber light and shadow. I closed my eyes and said, "You're not allowed to be mad at me. I was run over today, by a Dodge RAM."

"I'm not mad at you."

"But you will be in a minute."

"What are you talking about?"

"I want you to go via Rosedale and Gleason. I want to stop at the Reynoldses' on the way home to give them the news."

"Son of a bitch!"

"See? I told you. Not allowed."

"Ten minutes, Stone! We go in, we tell them, and we leave."

"Okay."

As we cruised up Rosedale, she asked me in a flat voice, "You don't want to go and see Chad too?"

"Uh-uh, that can wait till tomorrow. But I think we should get the Reynoldses' reaction straightaway."

She was quiet for a bit. When she spoke again, there was a curious frown in her voice. "What's on your mind, Stone?"

"A large whiskey."

"I'm serious!"

"I don't know, Dehan. I just want to see how they react." I still had my eyes closed. I put on my best English accent and added, "You know my methods, Watson. Apply them!"

"Dork."

We pulled up outside the Reynoldses' house, behind the white pickup truck. The back was covered in a blue tarp. We climbed out of the Jag and slammed the doors. My body felt like it was made of painful concrete. The rain had slowed to a heavy drizzle. As I squeezed past the hood of the Jag, I peered under the tarp on the pickup. Then we moved across the road and Dehan went ahead to ring on the bell. The door was opened after a moment by Samuel. He stared at us each in turn for a moment, then said, "We were eating."

Dehan answered. "We are sorry to disturb you. We have some important news about the case. We thought you and your dad would want to know straightaway."

He stepped back and said, "You'd better come in," and jerked his chin toward the living room that doubled as his father's bedroom. We went in. They had dark green drapes closed over the window, an old, electric fire burning, and a TV set up on the table so the old man could watch it from the bed. Samuel had a plate of meat and mashed potatoes on the floor beside his straight-backed chair. His father watched us come in with his mouth slightly open. "What's happened?" he said.

"Turn off the TV, Daddy. The detectives have some news for us."

He didn't wait for his father. He picked up the remote control and killed the TV. Then he sat on his hard chair but didn't pick up his plate. His dad watched Dehan sit on the sofa, and as I sat next to her, he scowled and said, "You sent a whole load of cops trampin' all over my baby's bedroom, takin' away sheets, making a whole mess up there. Lenny never made a mess like that! Gave me pain in my chest and sent my blood pressure right up. Samuel very nearly had to rush me to the ER."

I waited till he'd finished and said, "I'm very sorry about that, Mr. Reynolds. It's actually about Lenny that I wanted to talk to you." I glanced at Samuel. He was frowning hard. "He is now our prime suspect. My chief believes the case is all but closed."

Reynolds' mouth sagged. "*Lenny?* No! No, no! No! Not Lenny! You must be out of your minds. Lenny didn't kill my Celeste! He was crazy about her! Ever since she was born! He doted on her like an uncle. Like he was my own brother. We was practically family!"

I grimaced and glanced at Samuel again. He had gone pale. I said, "There is actually more to it than that. You both need to brace yourselves because this is bad news. Celeste and Lenny had been lovers for about six months before she was killed."

Samuel closed his eyes. "Sweet Jesus!"

His father was squinting, giving his head little shakes. "How could you possibly know a thing like that?"

Dehan said, "That's what those officers were doing in her room, Mr. Reynolds. They found traces of Lenny's semen on her sheets."

Samuel got to his feet. He looked suddenly huge, as though he had grown by a couple of feet. His voice boomed, "*Jesus, Mary, and Joseph, and sweet fuckin' Joanna! In our own fuckin' house! Under our own fuckin' roof!*"

His father almost screamed at him, "*Language, Samuel! You will not use that blasphemous language in my house!*"

Samuel's face went crimson. He stared hard at the wall and his jaw muscle bunched and pulsed like an artery. "Under our own roof!" he said again. "In our own house! It was God's punishment! She had no shame! May God forgive me! My own sister, and she had no shame! It was God who struck her down!"

I spoke quietly. "Sit down, Samuel." He frowned at me a moment, like I had asked him to do something unreasonable, and sat. "We also found her laptop at Chad Norris' house. When we checked her emails, it emerged that they had started seeing each other about six months earlier. The theory is that during that time, she met Chad and didn't know how to tell Lenny. On that Sunday evening, when she was on her way to Chad's house, she received a number of calls. One was from this landline, another was from Chad, but there were a couple of others that came from an unregistered phone belonging to Lenny. Our theory is that she broke it off with him that day, by phone. Later that evening, he called her from the station house while she was on her way to Chad's."

Reynolds had started shaking his head again.

I ignored him, watching Samuel, and continued. "He asked her to meet him at the Watson Gleason Playground. We have a number of witnesses who saw her meeting a man on that corner. The witnesses say the man turned up in a white truck, like Lenny's . . ."

Reynolds was suddenly half shouting, "No, no, no, no, no, Lenny did not do that! No! Don't tell me Lenny did that! He did not do that!"

His face seemed to fold in on itself, tears spilled from his eyes, and saliva ran from his mouth. He buried his face in his sheet, rocking and making appalling moaning noises that seemed barely human. "No, no, Lenny didn't do that. Ask him, for God's sake! He'll tell you you're all wrong."

"I'm afraid Lenny is in the hospital." I glanced at Samuel again. His eyes were wide. "We went to talk to him and he fled. He tried to leave the country. He pulled a gun on officers at the airport, stole a vehicle, and tried to drive away. There was an accident, and he is now in the operating theater at the hospital."

Samuel scowled at his sobbing father. "You'll say what you like, Daddy. You're always protecting her, but that girl had the Devil in her soul as sure as my name is Samuel Reynolds."

His father's voice was a sobbing squeak. "You'll not talk about your sister like that! She was misguided, a lost soul . . ."

"Evil is what she was and is. A black heart and a black soul!

You know it as well as I do, but you won't accept it! Look how she has you! Even from beyond the grave, she's destroying you! An old man before your time!"

"*Don't!* She was my little baby. She was your poor mother's parting gift to me when the Lord took her. She was a sweet angel of a child." His head dropped back on the pillow, his eyes squeezed tight, and his mouth opened, making him look oddly as though he was either dead or snoring. His body quivered. "She was my little girl."

Samuel's voice was shrill: "*Will you stop saying that! Can you not see she is destroying us all! She's killing you! She dwells still in Helen!*"

His father twisted on his side, turning his back to us, pulling the sheet with his fists to cover his face, kicking his feet like a small boy. He gave an odd, small scream, then, "*She's family! Family! She's your little sister! She's my baby girl!*"

Samuel stared at him with bulging eyes. Slowly, his face started to collapse, like his father's. Tears slipped from his eyes, and his bottom lip too curled in under his teeth. He spoke in a strangled, distorted voice. "How can you say that? She killed Mom. Before she was even *born*, she killed Mom! She lives now in Helen, driving her into madness . . ."

"*Don't say that!*"

"Look what she's doing to you! Family? We were a family, before she came and destroyed us all! She has the Devil in her heart. Even from the grave, she is killing us one by one! And you can't see it!"

Reynolds was whimpering, "Get out. Leave me alone. Get me a doctor. I'm dying. It's you killing me, not her. Leave me alone . . ."

I glanced at Dehan and stood, wincing with the pain as I straightened. Samuel was still staring at his father with bulging eyes, his mouth drawn down into an ugly, silent sob. Dehan stood too.

I said, "You'd better let him rest, Samuel. And call the doctor, to be on the safe side."

He stood and followed us silently into the hall, then turned to walk away toward the kitchen. I said, "Samuel, do you work with a partner?"

He frowned at me like the question was an insane one, then shook his head. "No, I work alone, like my dad before me." Then he added, almost by rote, "Don't see no sense paying out good money when I can do the work myself."

I nodded. "Sure."

He turned and continued on his way to the kitchen, and we made our way to the front door. As I was opening it, I became aware of a presence on the stairs and turned to look. Helen was standing halfway up, with her bare legs and feet caught in the light from the hall, but her upper body in semidarkness.

"Hello, Helen."

Her voice was unemotional. "Is Celeste killing us?"

"No. She's not."

"I thought, once she was dead, she couldn't hurt us anymore."

I nodded. "She can't. Good night, Helen."

"Good night."

We stepped out into the drizzle and closed the door behind us. The porch light made the wet concrete path shiny, but the street was mainly in darkness because the streetlamps were enclosed by the trees. I looked again at the white pickup with its blue tarp on the back, covering the plastic sacks of rubble. I stepped past it, and it occurred to me I must be getting old, because the sight of my ancient burgundy Jaguar, with its leather and walnut interior, was somehow calming and reassuring. I limped over to the passenger side and climbed in as Dehan got behind the wheel again. The doors clunked shut, and she put the key in the ignition.

"You ready to go home now?"

"I am."

"You sure you don't want to go and drop any more bombshells on any more dysfunctional families before bed?"

"Quite sure, Dehan. You can't deny," I said as she turned the key and the big engine roared into life, "that it was a very instructive exercise."

"Is that what they're calling it these days?"

She was quiet then all the way down Gleason until we turned left onto White Plains. Then she said, "Instructive." Not as a question, but as a statement.

I looked at her along my eyes without moving my head.

She said, "I don't know, Stone. How was it instructive?"

I watched a cluster of raindrops gather on the windshield, turning the world outside into a jumble of broken light and pictures. Then the wipers swept it away, so that the nocturnal street was clear again for a moment, until the drops started gathering once more.

"I'm guessing," I said, "that while we were there, you were feeling sullen and grumpy, and what you were focusing on was your desire to go home and have a bubble bath, surrounded by evil-smelling candles."

She raised a hand and grinned. "Guilty."

"I don't blame you, but now ask yourself. If you had not been focusing on that, but on them, what would you have noticed?"

"Okay, my bad. Let me think." She sighed. "The old man in deep denial about his daughter and Lenny."

"That old man is only ten or fifteen years older than me."

"That's what denial will do for you. What else? Samuel." She shook her head. "Man, that guy has a *lot* of pent-up . . ." She stopped. She drove in silence for a good two or three minutes. Finally she said, "Okay, you made your point. His motive is at least as credible as Lenny's and Chad's. He really hated his sister."

"Anything else?"

"Something else?" She thought for a bit. "Yeah," she said after a while. "He wasn't so much mad at the fact that she was having an affair with Lenny, as the fact that she did it under the family roof."

I nodded. "His dad didn't seem all that surprised. But he was outraged that they had done it in the house. Anything else?"

"Jeez, Batman! Uh . . . Well, yeah, the whole thing about how Celeste had been systematically destroying the family. She had the Devil in her heart . . ."

I grunted. "That's more of the same, Little Grasshopper. Anything else?"

She glanced at me. "Your weird, untimely question about whether Samuel worked alone? No, nothing else, but you obviously did."

I laughed softly. She slowed and turned right onto Morris Park Avenue.

"Oh, I noticed lots and lots, but there was one thing in particular I had hoped you had spotted."

"Go on, tell me."

"What was in the back of the white pickup?"

She went very still. "Uh . . . a blue tarp . . ."

"Under the blue tarp."

"I don't know, Stone. Jesus. You noticed?"

"Ooooh, Ritoo Glasshopper, Sensei notice everything!" I laughed painfully, then said, "It was full of those toughened plastic sacks that builders use. There must have been fifteen or twenty of them, all full of sand."

"Yeah? Is that important?"

"How heavy do you figure each of those sacks is?"

"I don't know, a hundred, hundred and ten pounds?"

"Could you heft fifteen or twenty of them into the back of a pickup truck?"

"Probably not."

"How about Lenny? You think he could? I know I'd find it hard work."

She was quiet for a long while. Then she lifted both hands off the wheel in a gesture of exasperation. "Come on, Stone! Okay, the guy is strong enough to heft a girl of ninety or a hundred pounds over a fence or a railway line and onto the riverbank. That is circumstantial *at best*! Lenny was having an affair with her! He concealed evidence! He ran when we went to get him! He shot at cops! He tried to run you down, for crying out loud! Come on, Stone! The guy is as guilty as a bishop in a whorehouse!"

I nodded silently a few times. "Lenny fired high and he swerved to miss me. He was reckless, he didn't aim to kill me. But maybe you're right. Maybe it was Lenny—I surely would like to know how he disposed of the body though, and why he did it so incompetently." I watched her face for a bit, bathed in soft amber, concentrating on the road. After a bit I went on, "Lenny has been on the force twenty years. Fifteen in homicide. How many murders do you think he has dealt with in that time?"

She sighed, slowed, and turned left into Haight Avenue. Then she pulled up in front of our house and killed the engine and the lights. The rain drummed softly on the roof.

I said, "He finds, suddenly, that in a fit of rage he has killed this girl, in the middle of the street. What does he do? He picks her up, carries her to his Jeep, and after all the homicides he has worked, instead of taking her to a remote, desolate place close to his home, like Ferry Hill or Castle Point, where the body will be carried out to the East River and probably never found again, he takes it to a highly populated area, where he has to carry it over difficult, wet, slippery objects and dump it in a river that will *not* carry it immediately out. What would make Lenny do something as stupid as that?"

"I don't know."

"Come on," I said. "You owe me a large whiskey and a curry."

We clambered out into the drizzle, put our arms around each other, and staggered up the steps to the front door.

FIFTEEN

Next morning brought with it more steady rain. The sky had changed from big, bellying, menacing watercolor clouds to a uniform ceiling of gunmetal gray. The wind had dropped, and with it the squally lash of raindrops had gone, replaced by the slow, steady tap of heavy drizzle and the splash of overflowing guttering. We got up late, around ten, though the dull light and lack of contrast suggested it could be anything between six a.m. and six p.m.

We made coffee in silence. She cooked bacon while I fried eggs and made toast. Then we sat and had breakfast, stared out the gray window, and felt sorry for ourselves. Finally, at eleven, while we were washing up, I said:

"I'm going to go and see Chad."

She dried her hands on a tea towel, gazing dreamily at the sodden lawn in the backyard, and said, "Why?" Then she blinked and looked at me, frowning. "What for?"

"Something happened that night, Dehan. We haven't got the whole picture."

She heaved a big sigh. "I know. I was thinking about it last night. I even dreamed about it." She shrugged. "You're right. As it stands, there is something missing in the picture. Lenny would not and *could* not have disposed of the body the way it was disposed of." She rested her ass against the sink. "Which means either he didn't do it, or he had an accomplice. If he didn't do it, it is really hard to explain his behavior at the airport."

I studied her face for a bit. After a moment, she asked me, "What do you think Chad can tell you?"

"What happened that night."

"How would he know, Stone?"

"Let's find out."

She looked unhappy. "I wish you'd let me in on your thought processes sometimes, big guy."

I grabbed my phone from the breakfast bar and spoke as I looked for his number and dialed. "There is no special thought process, Dehan. It just doesn't make sense that it went down the way people are saying it went down. So it must have gone down in a different way. And I have a hunch Chad knows more than he's saying, because his story doesn't quite make sense either."

We arranged to meet outside the law school on West 116th Street. We picked him up in the Jag and drove down Amsterdam to Friedman's, where we managed to park right outside and duck in out of the rain. The place was almost empty. We found a booth against the wall and ordered three burgers and three beers.

When the waitress had gone, Chad spread his hands. "You said you had news."

Dehan was quiet, watching me.

I nodded. "Detective Leonard Davis is in the hospital, in a critical condition. If he pulls through, he will be charged with Celeste's murder."

He frowned and looked down at his hands on the table. "A cop?"

"You don't know who Leonard Davis is."

He squinted at me and shook his head. "Should I?"

"He was the detective in charge of investigating Celeste's murder."

He made a face that indicated what he thought of cops in

general. "That's great. So why would this Davis want to kill Celeste?"

"It seems he was Rod."

I waited. I watched his eyes. They darted around the table with small, quick movements, like thoughts and memories were laid out there and he was reading and cross-referencing them, trying to make sense of them. A couple of times he gave a small frown.

Finally, I said, "What? That doesn't make sense to you?"

He shrugged. "I'm not the detective. You'll build your case and see what the jury makes of it."

"I'm curious what you make of it."

"I don't know what evidence you've got."

I watched his eyes carefully. "A white truck?"

He looked away at the empty tables and after a moment shook his head. "I don't know what you're driving at, Detective Stone. You're obviously trying to trap me or draw me into admitting something. I have no idea what it is. Why don't you just come out and ask me?"

I nodded. "What really happened that night, Chad?"

"I already told you."

"You told me half the truth."

"So you say."

"Here's my problem. Detective Leonard Davis and Celeste had been having an affair for about six months. She was wild, out of control. Then she met you. From what you have told me, and I believe you, you were very focused on building a career, and she liked that in you. I don't believe that back then, when you met her, you were the embittered cynic you pretend to be now. I think you both had chemistry and liked each other, and she felt she had found something in you. See, her dad and her brother are always talking about family, but actually Celeste had no family at all in any meaningful sense of the word. But I believe she felt she had found some kind of family in you. And I think that feeling was mutual. How am I doing?"

The waitress brought the beers and set them before us. As she walked away, Chad shrugged and made a face. "Pop psychology, a cop's gut, who cares? How is any of this relevant to anything?"

"It's relevant because, as you well know, about ninety percent of murders are motivated by love."

"You have the man you're going to charge, now you want to frame me?"

"No." I gave my head a small shake. "You see, I think, when you found out about Rod . . ."

"Detective Leonard Davis."

"When you found out about him, and read his text messages, I think that was a major blow to you. I think you felt hurt and betrayed."

"Okay, maybe I did, so what?"

"I think that's why instead of kicking her out, the way you kicked out your roommate, Nigel, without a second thought, you had a big, almighty row which ended, as you said, in makeup sex."

"Again, so what? I told you all of this already."

I nodded again. "And she told you, at least partly, who Rod was, and why she hadn't shaken him off yet. Am I right?"

He didn't answer for a bit. Then he said simply, "Yes. She didn't say he was a cop . . ."

"She told you he was an older man, a friend of the family, and that he'd helped her through a difficult time."

"Yeah."

"But then she promised she was going to break it off with him."

"Yeah."

"So she went home, telling you she'd be back that evening, but when it started to get late and she didn't show, you called her. What did she say?"

"Late Sunday morning, she said she was going to go home, collect a few things, call Rod—she said his name was Lenny—tell him she had met somebody and it was over with him. We were going to try living part of the week together and see how that went. She was going to get a job . . ."

"You were thinking of making a life together?"

"We were going to give it a go. When she wasn't crazy, she was great. She was smart, you know, actually intelligent. I thought we had a shot at making it work. But then it was getting late and she didn't show. So I called her. She said she'd spoken to him and broken it off. I asked her why she was late. She said she'd had a bad row with her dad and her brother. They'd called her evil, the Devil had a hold of her, and all kinds of crazy stuff like that. She'd been crying in her room and fallen asleep. But she said she was on her way and couldn't wait to . . ." He paused and sighed. "She couldn't wait to get home."

"It's a ten-minute walk from her house to yours. But she didn't show."

"I eventually called again. It was before nine. I was worried. She said she was actually walking, on her way, literally. I could hear that she was outside. She said Lenny kept calling. She also said her brother had called. Something in her voice made me worried. So I went to meet her."

I nodded. "That makes sense. What you told me before didn't make sense. Whichever way I tried to see it, you went to meet her. You had to."

"Yeah, I had to. I grabbed my keys and my coat and walked out. It was a two-minute walk to the playground, but when I got to the corner, I saw her, in her Red Riding Hood coat."

"Where?"

"At the playground."

"Where exactly?"

He sat back. His eyes became abstracted. "Memory plays tricks, but I'm pretty sure she was opposite the grocery store, in the shadow of the big tree there. She wasn't alone. There was a man there with her."

"Can you describe him?"

"Not in much detail. The light was poor. But Celeste was five-

five, and this guy was head and shoulders over her, a good seven to ten inches taller than she was."

Dehan spoke for the first time. "How can you be so precise?"

He took a deep breath and let out a shuddering sigh. "Because he was embracing her. He had his arms around her and they were swaying slightly side to side."

I raised a hand. "Let's be clear, Chad. You are saying that he was hugging her, not holding her by the shoulders?"

"No, no way. I was no more than fifty or sixty feet away. You can measure it. There are four big trees along there. I was standing by the second tree and I could see them clearly. He was holding her in his arms. Then he picked her up."

Dehan sounded incredulous. "He picked her up?"

"Yeah, like a groom carrying a bride over the threshold. He turned around and carried her back to the corner, to a white truck."

"What did he do next?"

"I don't know. I turned and went back home, and swore to myself that I would never trust another woman so long as I lived."

"Okay, Chad, I need you to be absolutely certain about your next answer. What kind of truck was it?"

"I can't tell you the make, but it was a pickup, maybe a Ford or a Toyota."

"Not an SUV with passenger seats in the back? A Jeep maybe?"

"No. It was a pickup."

The waitress arrived with our burgers, told us to enjoy our meal, and withdrew. I sat back, staring at my food, unseeing. I shook my head and said, "Chad, I don't know whether to tell you this or not. The man you saw was not Lenny, Rod, Detective Leonard Davis, whatever you want to call him."

His eyes narrowed. "Who the hell was it, then?"

"I'm not sure, but Detective Davis is about five foot six or seven at the most, and he drives a white Jeep Cherokee."

"Then I might have saved her?"

"I don't think so, Chad. I think by the time you saw them, she was already dead. I think what he did, after you turned away, was to put her in the back of the truck, under the tarpaulin. I'm sorry."

He was silent for a long time. None of us ate. Eventually he said, "So she didn't lie to me . . ."

It was Dehan who answered. "That has to be some kind of consolation, Chad."

He narrowed his eyes at her. "*Consolation?*"

"It sucks every way, Chad, but this way it sucks less, and at least you get to keep the memory."

The anger drained from his face. "It's cold comfort." He shook his head. "So are you going to charge Detective Lenny Davis?"

I said, "I don't know yet, Chad. To me, the case against him is getting weaker. Besides, we have no idea if he'll make it." Then I asked, "Chad, why didn't you tell us all this from the start?"

He looked surprised. "Are you kidding? I didn't find out for a couple of weeks or more that she had been killed. There was no evidence against anybody, and I was the last person to see her alive, after a quarrel because she had been unfaithful. At the very least, it would have meant a police investigation and a trial that would have ended my career before it had even begun. As far as I was concerned, she had betrayed me and screwed the wrong guy. End of story." Then he stared hard into my eyes. "You know who did this, don't you?"

I shook my head.

He said, "I have to go. Thanks for bringing me the news." He slid along the bench to stand up, then stopped and hesitated. "I'm sorry I got it wrong. I should have stepped up."

He left twenty bucks on the table to cover his lunch and walked out, hunching his shoulders into the rain.

I shifted around to Chad's seat, where I could see Dehan across the table, picked up his burger, and started eating it. Dehan watched me do it and said, "Boy, did we ever get it wrong."

I said, with my mouth full, "I never liked Lenny for the murder."

"I gotta hand it to you, Stone. You were right on the money." She picked up her own burger and bit into it. We stared at each other across the food, ruminating like two sheep. She swallowed and took a long pull on her beer, then showed her empty glass to the waitress and made a *V* sign with her fingers. After that she shifted her ass so she was sitting in the corner, looking at me and eating.

"So," she said after a while. "We have Chad and Celeste, post–infidelity trauma, in post–makeup sex bliss, and they promise each other that they are going to try to make it work. She is longing for the family she's been promised all her life by her crazy dad and brother, and he has these values he's learned from his dad—focus and commit! So between them, they are starting to build a dream. They are going to make a family."

I was nodding and chewing. I agreed with what she was saying.

She took a big bite out of her burger and spoke with her mouth full. "She gomph hom . . ."

"She goes home?"

"Mm-hm . . ."

I took over to give her the chance to eat for a while. "But Dad and Sam are, literally, as mad as hell. As far as they are concerned, her behavior over the last couple of days . . ."

"Lasht couple beers!"

"Last couple of years, indeed, has been sinful, wicked, even evil. There is an unspoken, perhaps even unadmitted, perception in the family that Celeste killed her mother. Dad denies it furiously: she is his baby girl. But Sam certainly believes it, and so does Helen. I get the impression that there is an idea that Helen was driven into her psychotic state by her mother's death. In short, Celeste is held responsible for all the evil that has befallen that family."

I took another bite of my burger. Dehan took a swig of beer

and pulled the third burger over to her. "You want to share?" I shook my head and chewed. She went on. "So if her behavior until that point has been evil and sinful, that weekend she really crosses a line, staying out Friday night, Saturday night, and coming back late Sunday morning, probably talking about staying out Sunday night too. All hell breaks loose, in more senses than one. She goes upstairs, breaks up with Lenny over the phone, and cries herself to sleep."

"Chad calls."

"She tells him she is on her way. She has her second row and leaves. Now, Lenny calls her from the landline, telling her to come home. He is coming after her. She stops at the playground to wait for him because, as we have said before, she doesn't want Chad to witness what her crazy family are like. Lenny calls while she is waiting, but contrary to what we thought, she tells him to leave her alone—and he does. Chad calls. She says that she is almost home. Samuel turns up in his truck. Parks. She gives him a mouthful. They struggle, she starts screaming, and he chokes her to shut her up, or maybe because he is venting all the hatred and resentment he has stored up against her since she killed his mom. Suddenly, he snaps out of it and realizes what he has done. In a fit of grief and remorse, he hugs her. We know he's strong enough to hold her upright. And that is when Chad shows up and sees what he believes is Rod and Celeste in an embrace. Samuel picks her up in his arms and, as you said, carries her to the truck."

I finished my burger and sat licking my fingers and sucking my teeth. The waitress delivered my second beer and I took a pull. "Unless Lenny pulls through and can substantiate some of that, we haven't got a shred of evidence to support it, aside from some very weak eyewitness testimony. It is all circumstantial. How do we prove it?"

"We have one chance," she said. "We show how he disposed of the body. Maybe we can nail him if we can show how, and why, he disposed of the body the way he did."

I nodded. "Yup, I think you're right. We need to get back on that, even if it means going in person to each business along the river, one by one."

SIXTEEN

My phone pinged, letting me know I had an email, and a second later, it began to ring.

"Stone."

The inspector's voice said, "Ah, John, it's John."

"Good afternoon, sir."

"Indeed, listen, I have word from the hospital. Lenny is dead. He died this midday. They did all they could in surgery, but it seems the damage to his left lung was too extensive and he had lost a lot of blood. They couldn't save him."

"I'm sorry to hear that." I glanced at Dehan. She mouthed, *Lenny? Dead?* I nodded. She closed her eyes and buried her face in her hands. "Listen, sir, Dehan and I have been discussing the case, and we had a talk with Chad Norris, we think it isn't as clear-cut as . . ."

"You know, John, I am sure you're right, but there is more to be taken into account here than the minutiae of precisely what happened, how, where, and when. Not least is Lenny's wife and kids, who face a very harrowing time ahead. There is the impact on the department itself: questions will be asked by the media and also at a very senior level of the department, about how this could have happened, on *my* watch, and this will not be an easy time for me either."

"I understand that, sir, but the point is, we think it's possible that, though Lenny was having an affair with Celeste . . ."

"A girl who thankfully was of age, but barely so, and he in his late forties, old enough to be her father. The press will have a field day, and the last thing we need, John, is accusations of a cover-up or attempting to whitewash this case. We need to be up front, transparent, and honest. Heaven knows we do our best, but they don't realize it is impossible to one hundred percent eradicate corruption. Policemen and women are people, after all, at the end of the day!"

"Sir . . ."

"We are going to close the case, John. You and Dehan have, as always, done exceptional work. It is a shame that the guilty party was one of our own. But we must be brave and face it down."

"Sir . . ."

"Yes, John."

"I don't think Lenny did it."

He was quiet for a moment. "I appreciate that, John, but we just have to roll with this one."

"No, I don't think you understand, sir. We are actually convinced that Lenny did not do it. He couldn't have . . ."

"John, the case is closed. I've had someone notify Mrs. Davis. We'll keep our heads down, and with a little luck, the storm will blow over."

"Sir . . . ?"

"Take a few days off, and I'll see you back here next week."

He hung up.

Dehan was looking at me with her hands in front of her mouth like she was praying. I could see the tears in her eyes. I said, "You okay?"

She nodded once, then asked, "What's going on?"

"The inspector closed the case. Lenny goes down as a murderer, and his wife and kids have to live with that." I shook my head. "He was a rat and a cheat, and I don't condone what he did, but he wasn't a murderer."

She sighed and her breath was a little unsteady. "He almost was, John."

I shook my head again, more emphatically. "No, Dehan, and I speak as his intended victim. Celeste was murdered. In the airport, he believed he was fighting for his life. What he did was stupid, but it wasn't murder in the way that Celeste was murder."

She frowned at me for a long time. "That's a discussion that will have to wait for a bottle of wine and a couple of whiskeys in front of the fire. Right now, we have a chief who is about to make a very serious mistake. What are we going to do about it?"

"He's put us on leave till next week. What we are going to do is ignore him."

"How?"

I grunted. "We could start by going to give the Reynoldses the news."

She screwed up her nose and thought about it. "Provoke Sam into discussing his sister? Get him really mad and see if he admits it?"

I shrugged with my eyebrows. "As a family, they are not hard to provoke. You could leave me alone with the dad and take Samuel off to one side, talk to him in confidence about Lenny, make him feel that you would understand how somebody might feel with a sister like that . . ."

"It could work, but it's a real long shot. He's not big at opening up with women either. May be better if you spoke to him." She jerked her head at my phone. "What was the email?"

"Probably another list of names from the riverside businesses. I've had three so far and the names mean nothing." I pulled out my phone and opened the message. I started to read, frowning. "Blackstone's Builders, no job too big or too small . . ."

"Spam?"

I shook my head. "No, I was looking into extending the house into the backyard . . ." I looked up at her. "You know, for the kid's room."

She gaped and I laughed. "I don't know what it is, let me read it. 'Dear Detective Stone, further to your yadda yadda, attached is a list'—another list of personnel." I glanced at her. She was still gaping, but now she was smiling too. "Four down, only ninety-six to go. P. O'Mally, E. Brown, J. Fenlon, W. Codey, C. Clay, nana, nana, nana . . ." I skipped through the names. There were about thirty of them. Then, near the end, I saw it. I slid the phone across the table to Dehan. She read it out loud:

". . . S. Reynolds."

"Let's go talk to them."

Blackstone's Builders was on Bronx River Avenue, a hundred and fifty yards from Westchester Avenue Bridge. It consisted of a big yard, maybe a hundred and fifty feet across and seventy-five or a hundred feet deep. It was fenced off from the road with a chain-link fence, but the other three walls were improvised out of sheets of corrugated steel that had started going rusty, and the far wall was overgrown with bramble and trees reaching over from the riverbank beyond.

The yard was strewn with building materials, and there were several trucks, a long warehouse, and, in the far right corner, a two-story building that overlooked the site. It was made of wood and had an outside staircase leading to the upper floor.

We pulled up on the muddy gravel just outside that building and made our way at a slow run to the main door. A bell rang as we pushed in, hunched into our coats, and closed the door behind us. There was a desk painted green with a smiling woman sitting behind it, watching us. And there was a man in a red V-neck jumper with a large, black moustache, leaning on the desk with his elbow, also watching us and smiling.

"Nice motor," he said. "How can we help you?"

I showed him my badge. Before I could say anything, he said, "Aha, Detectives Stone and Dehan, of the Forty-Third. You're here about our employees of 2016." He held out his hand. "Geoff Blackstone. This is my wife, Kathleen. I am not sure how helpful we can be, Detectives, we use a lot of casual and part-time labor. It's the nature of the business."

Dehan said, "We are particularly interested in one employee. Anything you can tell us . . ."

"Come through to my office. Kath, make us some coffee, would you?"

"Of course, Mr. Blackstone!"

They both hooted with laughter, and he led us through to a very basic office with one small window that overlooked the yard. He had a gray, steel desk with a black, imitation leather chair behind it and two blue chairs where he indicated Dehan and I should sit as he lowered himself into his vinyl throne.

"Who is the employee you are interested in, Detectives?"

Dehan answered. "Samuel Reynolds."

He thought for a moment, gazing at the ceiling. "Yes, I recall him. He worked for us on and off for a long time. Big man, strong, good worker. Very devout, as I recall. Sam, Sam Reynolds. He never had a long-term contract, though we did offer one. I seem to remember he hoped to start up his own business. I can only imagine he was eventually successful, because he stopped coming to us and we have never seen him again."

"But before 2016 he worked for you on a regular basis?"

"Yes, a few months on, a couple of months off . . ."

There was a knock at the door and Kathleen Blackstone came in with three cups of coffee on a tray. We thanked her, and Geoff barked with mock severity, "That'll be all, Miss Blackstone!" and they both roared again as she left the office.

Dehan's mouth gave a thin smile while her eyes thought about something else. "Did Reynolds ever have a key to the premises, Mr. Blackstone?"

He frowned like the idea was absurd. "Good grief, no. He was just casual labor. A good worker, but he didn't enjoy our trust."

"Can you think of any way that he might have gained access to the premises in November of that year?"

He frowned at his desktop for a while, then bellowed, "*Kathleen!*"

She leaned in, smiling. "Yes, dear?"

"Remember the break-in, couple of years ago?"

She nodded. "Mm-hm . . ."

"When was that?"

Her eyes seemed to scan the ceiling, as though she had an invisible calendar pinned up there. "That was the night of Sunday, the sixth of November. I remember because it happened on a Sunday, when we were not here, and it was the week Trump was elected."

Dehan looked at me and her eyes were alight. Her face said, "This is it!" Geoff was saying, "You are a marvel, Kathleen! Isn't she extraordinary! It was an odd business, to be sure. We were having trouble with the alarm system. Basically, it was going off all the time, either because some bum wanted to sleep in the yard, a fox or a cat slipped through, or any number of other reasons. In the end, we decided to set alarms inside instead, where we stored the valuable gear, and simply have a solid padlock on the fence. We had, after all, never been broken into. This was back in 2014. We left the signs saying there was an alarm system, CCTV, and dogs, but what we actually had was alarms on the office and on the warehouse, and CCTV on the inside of those buildings, where it might be of some use.

"Well, on November sixth, somebody cut through the chain, let themselves in, stole absolutely nothing, and left without disturbing a damn thing. It was quite bizarre."

I leaned forward with my elbows on my knees. "Mr. Blackstone, this is extremely important, is there any direct access to the river from this yard?"

He looked mildly astonished. "Why, yes! The boys loosened a

couple of panels over in the corner, years ago, and made a kind of doorway out onto the riverbank. It's rather pleasant out there and they have an area set up for their lunch breaks and coffee breaks in summer and spring." He laughed. "Management are not allowed, but I believe they actually have a refrigerator out there in hot weather. I am happy to let them enjoy it . . ."

"Could we see it, please?"

Now he looked worried. Kathleen was still at the door. She looked worried too. He said, "Well, yes, of course, but I am sure they are not breaking any laws . . . are they?"

I shook my head. "No, please, just point us in the right direction and we'll find our way."

"It will be frightfully muddy at the moment."

I smiled. "Will you show us where it is, please?"

He led us out of the office again, back to the front door, and pointed through the glass, across the muddy yard, to a section of the corrugated steel in the corner, about forty yards away. It was heavily overgrown with creepers and bramble, but I could just make out that one of the sheets did not fit snugly.

"You see the one that is protruding slightly? Well, if you tug on that, it leads out to a rather flat, grassy area which is a part of the riverbank. The boys have set it up . . . Well, you'll see when you go out there. You don't need me to come along, do you?"

Dehan shook her head, and we stepped out of the small reception and once again into the drizzle. We squelched the forty or so paces through the mud and puddles with our collars turned up and finally came to the corner of the yard. The loose sheet of steel was now clearly visible, as were the improvised hinges in the corner, made from bent wire looped through holes punched in the edge of the sheet. I took hold of it, pulled it back, and hitched it open. Dehan crouched, peered through the opening at the rich, abundant, wet grass on the other side, and stepped over the threshold. I followed.

We were on a shoulder of land that protruded into the water. The river itself was barely visible because of the thick growth of ferns, grasses, brambles, bushes, and trees that swarmed along the edge. To the left, the shoulder ended abruptly beyond an elder tree and plummeted twelve or fifteen feet down to the dark water of the river. To the right, the shoulder tapered into a narrow path that skirted the fences and buildings, following the course of the river upstream toward the bridge. Ahead of us, it was just a tangle of undergrowth, obscuring the river from view.

Looking back on either side of the improvised gateway, I saw there were old plastic chairs, a table made out of wooden boxes, and signs that, in the summer, there was probably a portable fridge hooked up to the mains there. No doubt they stored water and fruit juice in that fridge.

Dehan stood awhile with her hands in her pockets, looking at the dense undergrowth. She started talking without looking at me.

"This is the answer to your question. He is not a criminal mind. He is not imaginative or very intelligent. He is a very simple man, and he works at a place—there must be a dozen like this—that has access to the river, where workers come on their lunch and coffee breaks, to relax and crack a surreptitious beer.

"When it dawned on him that he had killed his sister, he must have panicked, dumped her in the truck, and the first thing that came to his mind was to bring her here, weigh her down with rocks and rubble, and dump her in the river. It couldn't have been easy. He would have had to clear a path through all that . . ." She jerked her head at the undergrowth. ". . . to make sure she didn't get caught in the brambles and branches. But having done that, all he had to do was let her slide and sink."

I nodded, though she couldn't see me. After a moment, she started talking again.

"She must have lain down there, in the cold water, for almost a week. He couldn't face coming here, so he left his job. And eventually, the combination of the current, the gases in her decomposing body, and the improvised nature of the weights he must have used all eventually released her and allowed her to float downriver."

She turned to look at me at last, with the rain trickling down her face. I wiped the rain from mine with my hand. She said, "This is what you foresaw when we went to look at the place where she was found."

I shrugged. "Part of it."

"What do we do now?"

"We go and we tell the inspector what we've found. If he still insists on closing the case, we tell him we'll go to the press and the TV networks."

"Okay. And then we bring Sam in for questioning."

I nodded. "Let's go talk to the inspector."

SEVENTEEN

When we got there, he was on the phone. We could hear him through the door. I rapped with my knuckles but didn't wait for a reply. I opened the door and pushed in. Dehan closed it behind us. Deputy Inspector John Newman's face was an adrenaline-fueled slideshow of emotions, from anxiety and distress at what he was hearing on the phone to outrage at our entering unbidden and concern at not wanting to upset us. His eyebrows went up and down, his mouth opened and closed, his eyes widened and narrowed. He drew breath. He held it. He sighed.

Then, he dropped into his chair, closed his eyes, and said, "Yes, sir. I will be sure to do that. Yes, sir . . . Yes, sir . . . Indeed. I'll do that."

He hung up, raised his eyes, and stared up at me. I stared down at him and said, "Sir, I don't think I made myself clear on the phone. Lenny did not kill Celeste Reynolds."

He took a deep breath, held it, closed his eyes, and flopped back in his chair. Without opening them, he said, "Based on what, John?"

It was Dehan who answered, "Based on the fact that a smart cop with Lenny's experience of homicides in the Bronx would not in a million years have gone to the unnecessary trouble—and risk —of dumping a body upriver. Sir, there *is nowhere* to dump a body upriver without running a huge risk of getting caught. Plus in November, up there, with the rain, the cold, and the dark, access to the river is very difficult. Carrying a hundred-pound deadweight, it would be virtually impossible. Lenny, just like any other homicide cop in the Bronx, would know instinctively to dispose of the body south, in one of the parks, where access is easy and the currents feed directly into the East River. Stone saw this from the start and I ignored him."

He sighed again. "That is sound theory, but only theory, and we have the very real, practical *fact* that Lenny ran and tried to kill you—and a number of other cops as well. It is as good as a confession."

I drew breath, but Dehan was off again. "It's not just a theory, sir, we have facts to back it up. We started canvassing the businesses along the banks of the Bronx, south of Starlight Park, north of where she was found. Stone's theory was that the killer must have had a connection with one of those businesses, otherwise it made no sense to dispose of the body there. This morning, just after Stone talked to you, he got an email from Blackstone's Builders, on Bronx River Avenue, with a list of personnel, full time and part time, from 2016."

"...and...?"

She said, "Samuel Reynolds was employed there on a part-time basis in November. Not only that, sir, but the employees have an improvised gate to the riverbank, where they take their lunch, coffee, and cigarette breaks. Sunday night, November sixth, 2016, there was a break-in. Nothing was taken, nothing was disturbed."

"Dear God..."

"And that's not all..."

"More?"

I spoke before she could continue. "We interviewed Chad again, sir. I felt sure we were missing something about that night.

His behavior didn't make sense. And it turned out that he did go out to meet Celeste after he phoned her, contrary to what he had told us before. He said he saw her being embraced by a big, tall man, who then picked her up and carried her to a white pickup truck. At that point, he turned away and returned home, believing she had hooked up with Rod, her lover. So he didn't see what this man did with Celeste. He was sure the man was well over six foot because, as he embraced Celeste, he could see the height difference. Lenny and Celeste are about the same height, and his truck is not a pickup."

Dehan finished for me. "Samuel is over six foot, he is tall and very strong, and he has a white pickup."

He spread his hands. "It is very, very compelling . . ."

Dehan shook her head. "Sir, it is just about conclusive. All we need is his confession, and I am pretty sure we can get that."

"But how in hell do you explain Lenny's behavior?"

I sighed. "Sir, it is pretty simple. Chad did the same thing. And they were both right, to some extent. If Lenny had followed the evidence, he would have become the prime suspect in his own investigation. Logically, he must have known better than anyone that finding the real killer, once his colleagues had zeroed in on him and discovered his relationship with Celeste, was going to be almost impossible. He knew, as he told Frank, that the chances of there being any forensic evidence from the body, after a week in the water, were close to nil, but the circumstantial evidence against him was very strong. What he needed to do was kill the investigation as quickly and effectively as possible. That's why he told Frank not to bother with the glue chamber, that's why he didn't call the CS team to her room, or bother chasing up witnesses or going to see Chad.

"After we found the computer and took the sheets in for DNA testing, he assumed we'd go after him—and he panicked. But even so, he was shooting to scare, sir, not to kill, and he swerved to avoid me at the last minute. He just lost control."

The inspector and Dehan spent a moment nodding quietly.

Finally, he said, "Yes, put like that. Very well, John, what do you want to do?"

"We need to talk to the Reynoldses. We need to bring them in and interview them in depth."

They both frowned at me, like weird reflections of each other. The inspector echoed me: "The Reynoldses? The whole family?"

"Yes."

Dehan said, "Even Helen? She's crazy!"

The inspector looked momentarily scandalized. "She is suffering a mental illness, surely, Detective Dehan!"

I said, "It would be useful to have an interview with her, sir, with her psychiatrist present to evaluate her answers. While medicated, I think she is quite coherent."

"What exactly do you hope to get from this poor woman?"

I sighed. "From what I have been able to observe, she is aware of what happens in the house, she overhears conversations, and she is aware of how Celeste was perceived by her family. As I understand it, her slide into psychosis may have started when her mother died. She made a comment to me about her sister killing her mother. She may well know what happened the night Celeste died."

Dehan had been frowning throughout our exchange. Now her frown deepened. "Are you thinking of Helen as a suspect?"

I returned the frown, then shrugged. "Do you know who killed Celeste?"

Her eyes went wide. "I'm pretty sure it was Samuel!"

I smiled, a little exasperated. "I know you're sure of that, but do you *know* who killed Celeste?"

". . . No, of course not."

"Neither do I." I turned to the inspector. "We don't want to make the Lenny mistake again, sir. I'd like to be thorough and meticulous. I would like to bring all three of them in and question them in depth in light of the new evidence, and then compare their testimony."

He sat for a moment with his lips in a tight line and his

eyebrows high on his forehead. After a moment, he shifted his eyes to look at Dehan. "I think we have just been schooled, Carmen. What about the father? I understand he is bedridden."

"We can talk to his physician and have him or some other medical practitioner present to make sure he's okay."

"Very well, John. Go ahead and bring them in."

On the way back down the stairs, Dehan gave me a frown that had more than a touch of reproach in it. "Way to slap me down, Sensei! Was that necessary?"

I didn't answer straightaway. We pushed through the doors and stood on the porch for a moment, watching the rain fall. She said, "Will November never end?"

"I'm sorry, Dehan. I didn't intend to slap you down. I'm sorry it came across that way. Lenny almost killed several people through jumping to assumptions. In the end, he was killed, and had he not been killed, he would have been wrongly prosecuted, and possibly sentenced to life in prison, through cops jumping to conclusions that seemed obvious but were wrong. I agree with you that the evidence against Sam is almost overwhelming. But when I ask myself if I *know* that he did it, I have to answer that I don't. Do I know that Helen *didn't* do it? No, I don't."

She crossed her arms and looked down at the spray bouncing off the blacktop. "How tall is she?"

"Five ten, maybe five eleven."

"Is she strong enough? How would she know about Samuel's workplace . . . ?"

I burst out laughing. "I don't know, Dehan! That's why we need to talk to her!"

"Okay! Okay! I get it!"

"Come on, this is in for the duration, we have to make a dash for it."

As I said it, the door behind me opened and Maria, the desk sergeant, leaned out. "Detective Stone, there's a call for you."

"Who?"

"Father Arundel."

"*Who?*"

"Father Arundel, of the Blessed Sacrament Church."

Dehan screwed up her brow. "Isn't that the church opposite the Reynoldses' house?"

"Yeah." I turned back to Maria. "I'll take it at my desk, Sergeant."

Dehan followed me to the detectives' room. We both sat, and I put the phone on speaker.

"Father Arundel, Detective Stone here. What can I do for you?"

"Oh, I am very glad to hear from you, Detective. Your desk sergeant feared you might have left already."

"We were on our way to the Reynoldses' house, just opposite you."

"Oh, indeed? Well, it was about that that I was calling, Detective."

"You have some information that might help our investigation?"

"Not exactly, but uh . . . Samuel is here, in the church, right now, with his sister . . ."

I waited. I could hear his breathing. "Father? Are you all right?"

"It's, uh . . . He's here with his sister, Helen . . ." His voice was unsteady. "And he is up at the altar, holding a kitchen knife to her throat, and he says he will kill her if you do not come immediately and do God's will."

Dehan and I were staring at each other across the phone. Mo had stopped what he was doing at his desk and was staring over at us both. I said, "He wants me to go to the church and do God's will?"

"That is correct, Detective."

"And what is God's will? What is it I have to do?"

"Well, what is God's will and what Samuel *believes* is God's will may not necessarily be the same thing. However, I have no doubt he will tell you just as soon as you get here, which I hope will be sooner rather than later, Detective Stone."

"We're on our way, Father. Keep talking to him, and try to sound calm, like everything is okay."

"Very well."

Dehan raised an eyebrow and smiled. "Have faith, Father. Everything is God's will."

I hung up and we stood. Mo's mouth was slightly open as he watched us. I studied him for a moment with a slight frown. "Have you much experience with hostage situations on church altars, Mo, where you are required by the hostage-taker to do God's will? Any advice for me?"

He shook his head and his bottom lip wobbled slightly.

"Damn!" I said. "I was sure you were my guy. Catch you later, dude."

As we were reaching the door, he said, "Yeah, later . . ."

We ran down the steps and through the rain to the Jag. I backed out of the lot and skidded left onto Story Avenue, then accelerated through the downpour toward Rosedale. Dehan said, "You want backup?"

I shook my head. "No, I don't want to spook him. But hold that thought. Things could change pretty fast."

"How do you want to handle this?"

"Try to help him relax and come down. He's having a crisis. Let's help him through it. We'll talk and find out what's going on in his mind."

"He wants to talk to you. What do you want me to do?"

"Stay close. If things get out of hand, call for backup. Don't draw your piece unless you're absolutely sure he's going to hurt Helen—or somebody else."

She nodded, then glanced at me sidelong. "You might be able to draw a confession out of him."

"You never know."

I skidded onto Rosedale and then sped north with hazards

flashing and leaning on the horn. Dehan asked, "Haven't you got a siren?"

"Yeah, I'm using it."

"Jesus, Stone! Get a damned siren!"

The tires complained turning right into Watson, but the Jag clung to the road like a freaked cat on a tiled floor. Then I jumped the lights onto Beach Avenue, took my hand off the horn, and cruised to a stop outside the church. The iron gate was open, as were the big, wooden doors set in the stone Tudor arch.

We ran through the rain and up the stone steps into the vast, domed interior. It was more like a small cathedral than a church, with great, towering arches reaching high into the vault above, and a domed copula over the altar. Behind the altar, the wall gleamed with gold leaf, and a vast crucifix was suspended from the wall, with that symbol of Man's eternal suffering, the tragic figure of Jesus, nailed, weeping and bleeding, to the wood. All around him, rich, elaborate statues and paintings adorned the walls and recesses, and candles flickered, illuminating his eternal punishment for that which he had never done.

I couldn't see Samuel or Helen, or the priest. I called out, "*Father Arundel?*" and my voice echoed and seemed to roll around the vast nave. Among the echoes, another sound added itself to the din. It was like a scrape, or a footfall, and the priest's figure appeared beyond the altar, rising from a crouching position.

He stood, backlit by the candles and the lamps and the reflections from the gold. He called, "*Detective Stone?*"

I said, "*Detectives Stone and Dehan!*"

And the two questions and the statement ricocheted against each other, climbing high into the cold vault.

He stepped a little closer. I still couldn't see his face. Behind me I could hear only the cold spatter of water, and I could feel the touch of cold air on my ankles and on the back of my neck.

"Will you approach? Samuel is here."

My footsteps reverberated, tapping like a clock, and Dehan's made a strange counterpoint, almost like a train leaving a station in the dark. Now his face came into view, partly illuminated by the candles. He was a man of about fifty, with thin, sandy hair. He looked drawn, worried, with hollow eyes. It was the face of a man called upon to solve a human problem, when all his life he had relied on God to solve them for him.

I stopped at the base of the altar and looked up. "Where is he?"

"He is prostrate."

"Where is Helen?"

"She is also prostrate."

"Does he know I am here?"

He nodded. "He is just finishing his prayers."

I sighed and raised my voice: "*Samuel! You said you wanted to talk to me. I'm here! Let Helen go and tell me what you want!*"

The padre peered behind him, then backed away. There was movement. Samuel emerged from behind the altar. He towered over us, looking down. In his left hand, he held Helen by the hair and forced her to kneel. In his right hand, he held a huge kitchen knife that gleamed and glimmered in the reflected light of the candle flames.

"She is a whore like her sister. God will exact his judgment. And you . . . !" He pointed at me with the long blade. "*You will be the instrument of His justice!*"

EIGHTEEN

"If I am the instrument of God's justice, Samuel, then hear my words and lay down your knife, and let Helen come here to me."

His voice was shrill: "*Satan speaks in you! You will betray the Lord! You will not punish her!*"

Helen was rigid on her knees, staring at nothing. I held up my right hand. "Slow down, Samuel." I looked at the padre. "Get out of here, Father." He scampered gratefully away. I looked back at Samuel. "Did you just say that I am the instrument of the Lord's justice?" He didn't answer. He stared with bulging eyes and swallowed repeatedly, with his Adam's apple moving up and down in his throat. "If I am the instrument of the Lord's justice, then you must have faith, Samuel, that I will do God's will. Let Helen come to me . . ."

He shook his head. "No! I can hear it in your voice. The Lord has made me wise. Satan's evil has been visited on our family and He has made me wise to it, to see the evil and excise it! You are lying to me. I can hear it in your voice."

I went to the front pew and sat. Dehan moved back and sat in the shadows across the aisle. I spread my hands and then laid them on my knees. "All right, Samuel, you tell me what it is I have to do."

"The evil is in her," he said.

"So you say, but what do you want me to do?"

"It was in her sister."

"And *your* sister, Samuel."

"She brought the evil into the world, and she killed Momma." His bottom lip curled in under his teeth. Tears spilled from his eyes, soaking his cheeks. He spoke in a choked, nasal voice, like he had flu. "She took Momma from us . . . She went into her belly and killed her. She went and she never came back . . ."

He yanked on Helen's hair. It must have hurt, but Helen didn't react. She looked catatonic. "*It was her fault!*"

"That is not Celeste, Samuel. That's your sister, Helen."

"*She has the evil in her! She killed Momma and she put her evil poison into Helen! She must be punished!*"

"So you keep saying, Samuel, but you won't tell me what it is I have to do."

"You are a policeman."

"Yeah."

"Then you must execute the law!"

"How?"

He pointed the big knife at his sister. She still seemed to be paralyzed, staring unseeing. "Kill her!"

I smiled, looked at the floor, and sighed again. "That is never going to happen, Samuel." I looked up at him. "God said, in the sixth commandment, remember? Thou shalt not kill."

"Unless the Lord ordains it. Jesus himself said, Matthew 15:4, 'He who speaks evil of father or mother, let him surely die.' She has the Devil inside her, she killed her mother and has brought her father low, crippled and broken him. She must die."

"That is not Celeste, Samuel. That is Helen. You can't punish Helen for Celeste's crime. You have to let her go."

He leaned forward, thrusting his face toward me. His voice was a rasp. "But she is *inside* her! She has gone inside her and made her sick! She is eating her mind, putting worms in her brain, making her crazy! She is killing her soul! She will kill us all!"

I spoke loudly. "Did you stop to think maybe she is doing that to you? The only person here threatening to kill anybody is *you*. *You* brought a weapon into the house of God. *You* are the one talking about killing, Samuel, not Helen."

He was shaking his head before I'd finished, stepping toward me, dragging Helen with him, making her stumble onto her hands and knees. "Not me! Not me! *You!* You are the instrument of God. You are the one who must execute his will. You are the one who must kill her and release her soul . . ."

I stood. "Okay. How do you want me to do this?"

He hesitated. A small click echoed around the church as Dehan cocked her weapon. He glanced over in her direction. I spoke again, drawing his attention back. "Come on, Samuel! I keep asking you, but you won't answer. What do you want me to do?"

I could see his hands were shaking. "She must be excised . . ."

"How?"

"You are God's instrument . . ."

His lip was curling in and he had started sobbing again. I moved toward the altar. "You want me to come up there and do it?"

He nodded miserably. "No tricks . . . It must be the will of God. You must do His will . . ."

"I plan to."

I didn't rush. I walked deliberately. I climbed the steps to the altar and stood just four or five feet away from him, with Helen on her knees between us, staring at nothing with huge eyes. I held out my hand. "I'll take it from here."

He stared feverishly at me. "What are you going to do?"

"Come on, Samuel. You told me I am God's instrument. Hand her over. I am going to lift her onto the altar, so it will heal and sanctify Helen's soul and release her from Celeste's Satanic hold."

"She must die . . ."

"I'm coming to that: then I will plunge the knife into her heart so that Celeste dies and is cast back into hell."

He started shaking his head. The action was almost frenzied, almost convulsive. He started saying, "No . . . ! No . . . !" his tone rising at the end, almost like a question.

I held out my hand, aware Dehan must be lining him up. I said, "Come on, Samuel. Let's get this over with. Let me take it from here."

His voice was becoming hysterical, verging on a scream. "*No . . . ! No . . . ! You're lying! You're lying! She's in you too! She's everywhere! She's everywhere! Oh, God in heaven, have mercy on me!*"

I lunged for him and grabbed his knife arm, pushing Helen away with my foot as I did it. But he was immensely strong and she barely moved. He slashed with his arm and I saw thick blood ooze from her neck. She toppled sideways and lay motionless. I bellowed, "*Get a medic!*"

Then he hurled me away and I fell, staggering backward down the steps, sending two tall, brass candlesticks crashing to the stone floor. The air was knocked painfully from my lungs, and I staggered gasping to my feet as he vaulted the barrier to the altar and ran toward the door, screaming for God to help him. I went after him, hearing his pleas echoing over my head as he plunged through the arched door, out into the rain.

I forced my bruised, aching body to sprint and burst out after him. The rain lashed into my face. Through the churchyard trees, I saw Samuel's hunched, lanky body racing toward his house. I went after him. He plunged through the gate and up the stairs. I was halfway across the road when he pushed open the door and went in. He slammed it as I followed. I swore under my breath, but I didn't hesitate. I knew Dehan had skills in the lock-picking department, but there was no time for that. There was no telling what Samuel might do in this frame of mind. I pulled my piece and blew out the lock with a single shot. Then, I kicked the door open and went in.

The house was dark and still. I called out, "Samuel? Where are you?"

There was no reply. I ran through possible locations in my mind: his bedroom, Helen's room, Celeste's room...

I remained motionless, listening for the slightest sound. I heard nothing. Then, suddenly, I knew where he was, the logical, natural place for him to go. I moved to the living room and opened the door. They were both sobbing like a couple of kids. Samuel was on his knees beside his father's bed, holding his father's hand in both of his own. His face was pressed onto it, and he was weeping, begging for his father's forgiveness.

His father had his face turned away, his other hand clasped over his eyes, and he too was sobbing. I stood in the doorway, watching them and listening to Samuel.

"I'm sorry, Daddy, I'm sorry. She had the Devil in her. You know she had the Devil in her. You said it yourself, didn't you? We both knew it."

The old man had started keening, shaking his head, and squeezing his eyes. All he kept saying, over and over, was, "Oh, Jesus, Sammy . . . Oh, Jesus! Oh, sweet Jesus . . . !"

Samuel raised his head from the bedcovers, hugging his father's arm and hand to his chest.

"She was killing us all, Daddy! You know she was! You said it yourself! She was going through us one at a time. She would have killed you. Sure! She's nearly killed you already! I had to do something! *I had to do something!*"

The old man looked up at the ceiling. His face was bright where the dull light from the window reflected off the tears that drenched his face.

"Sweet mother of God," he said. "Forgive me! What have I done to deserve this? What have I done to deserve this cruel punishment for my family? If I have done wrong, sweet Mother! Punish me! Don't punish my children like this!"

"Daddy, don't! Please, daddy, don't!"

I said, "All right! That's enough crazy ranting from both of you! What the hell is wrong with you, Samuel? You go storming into a church, demanding that an officer of the law murders an innocent woman? Get a grip, will you!"

He got to his feet and pointed a trembling hand at me. "You are an officer of the law. You need to get her out of here."

"There is an ambulance on the way that will take her to the hospital, and Samuel, you had better pray she comes through, or you are in serious trouble. You are coming with me to the station. We have a *lot* of talking to do."

Samuel swallowed. "To the police station?"

His father struggled onto one elbow, his mouth gaping. "I can't go to the station. I'm sick. I have angina . . . You can't."

"Your physician will be there. You can and you will. Both of you." Outside, I could hear sirens wailing far away, but drawing closer, and I knew Dehan had called for backup as well as an ambulance. I pointed at Samuel. "You, get your dad dressed and ready to come to the station. Do it now." I pointed at his dad. "You, don't move from this room."

I followed Samuel to the bottom of the stairs and watched him climb them to the upper floor, looking at me over his shoulder. He still looked crazy, but like maybe he was calming down. I turned and leaned out the front door. The ambulance had pulled up and two patrol cars with it. Blue-and-red lights were pulsing, leaping off the wet blacktop. I turned back to look up the stairs.

Samuel was standing, looking down at me. He reminded me of his sister before. His legs were illuminated by the dull, gray light from the open door, but his upper body and his face were in darkness. I could see he had a bundle of clothes held in his right hand, but he was standing immobile. I said, "Come on, Samuel. Cut the crazy act and let's get moving."

He came down the stairs one heavy tread at a time, but stopped right in front of me, staring deep into my eyes. He said, "You don't understand. She came from Satan. She brought evil to this house. She had to die."

"Who did, Samuel? Celeste? Are you telling me that you killed Celeste?"

He shook his head and said again, "You don't understand."

He moved along the hall and stopped as he opened his father's door. "I'm going to dress my father."

"Make it fast, Samuel."

He went in and closed the door.

I looked outside again and saw Dehan talking to the paramedics. They had a gurney they were wheeling toward the ambulance. I squinted and saw that Helen's head was not covered. She was alive. They lifted the gurney into the ambulance, climbed in, and closed the door. Then the ambulance was moving, wailing, heading toward the hospital.

Dehan approached the cops from the patrol cars, pointing up and down the road. I figured she was telling them to seal the area. Crime Scene would be on their way, but not, thankfully, Frank. This time, I told myself, nobody had died.

I turned and looked back at the door that had once been the living room door but was now the old man's bedroom door. There was silence. The whole damned house was silent. I wondered for a moment what it had been like for Celeste, a bright, intelligent young woman, imprisoned in this house, damned and condemned every day for having killed her mother, for being young, attractive, and free of spirit, assaulted verbally, insulted, humiliated, and damned to hell for wanting to experience life and love. There was no need to send her to hell, I told myself. She must already have been there.

Then the scream came. It was a scream, and a wail of grief and fear. I ran for the door and tried to push it open. It was locked. I hurled myself against it with my shoulder, kicked savagely at the latch. It wouldn't budge. Then I saw the smoke curling under the crack and shouted, "*Stand back! Stand away from the door!*" as I pulled my piece for the second time that afternoon, took aim at the lock, and fired. Then I kicked the door again and it smashed open.

The old man was curled up in the bed, covering his face with his arms, screaming and howling. Samuel was with him, clutching at him. He seemed to be trying to embrace him. His face was twisted with terror, but his voice was weirdly reassuring as he said over and over, "It's going to be okay, Daddy! We're going to heaven with Mom! We did the right thing! This is the right thing. We'll be okay now . . ."

And all around the room flames flickered, billowing toxic smoke. They licked up the curtains, they smoldered in the armchair, they made small explosions as they engulfed the sofa, and crackled and surged with blue flames as they crawled rapidly up the legs of the dining table and chairs. There was a soft roar of flames that grew louder as the room was steadily consumed.

I saw this all in a fraction of a second, and then I saw that the flames were creeping onto the bedcovers. I knew then that within minutes, the whole wooden house would be in flames, and I knew that within seconds, anybody in that room would be dead, first suffocated and then incinerated.

I ran in.

NINETEEN

I ripped the covers off the bed and grabbed the old man with both hands by the scruff of his neck. He was heavy, heavier than I had expected. Like all the Reynoldses, he was big. Billowing smoke was filling the room, belching from the drapes and the upholstery on the furniture, snaking from the varnished wood. I heaved again and dragged Reynolds toward me. He clawed at my arms and my shoulders, wailing incoherent noises and coughing violently.

I heaved at him a third time. He seemed impossibly heavy. My lungs were demanding air. Then I saw that Samuel was across the bed, dragging at his father, screaming at him, "*No, Daddy! You have to stay! This is our redemption! We have to be punished!*"

The heat was suffocating. The foot of the bed was now in flames. I dragged at the old man again and screamed at Samuel, "*Let go!*"

I covered my mouth with my arm as I breathed in, but the acrid smoke tore at my throat, making me cough. Reynolds was thrashing and kicking, fighting to get away from his son, retching and trying to cover his mouth and nose. The smoke was so thick I could barely see the door. A dull pain was splitting my head and I knew it was from lack of oxygen. I grabbed Reynolds with both hands again, and despair must have given me strength, because I dragged him off the mattress and onto his feet. Samuel was half on the floor, coughing violently between wailing and calling out to God to cleanse him of his sins.

Flames six feet high were engulfing the foot of the bed, wavering through the smoke. The heat was becoming intense. I knew I barely had seconds. Reynolds was clawing and clutching at me like a drowning man, dragging down his savior. He was at least as tall as I was and heavier. There was no way I could carry him. I shoved him and screamed in his face, "*Run!*" I pushed past him and he clung to me, dragging me back. Flames licked at our clothes. He was screaming in my ear, insane, incoherent noises. His arms were around my throat. My eyes were burning. I grabbed his arms, leaned forward so his feet were lifted off the ground, and charged for where I knew the door was.

I collided with a body. I heard Dehan shout, "*Stone!*" Then, hands were grabbing me, pulling me forward, and I fell in a heap in the hallway, with Reynolds on top of me. I pushed him off. Uniformed cops were seizing him, hauling him up and out of the house. I clambered to my feet, coughing and retching. Dehan was there, pulling on my arm. "*We have to get out!*"

"*Did you call the Fire Department?*"

"*Yes! Come on!*"

I shoved her toward the door. "*Go!*"

I ran down toward the kitchen. I turned the kitchen taps on full and filled a red plastic basin with water. I tipped it over my clothes and hair, soaked a tea towel, and tied it around my nose and mouth, and another around my head. Dehan was beside me, clutching my arm, screaming at me, "*What the . . . ? For crying out . . . ! No, Stone! No!*"

I wrenched my arm free and ran. I think I was bellowing like a demented demon. I plunged into the room, hearing the wet tea towels hiss and steam on my face. The smoke was a dense fog.

Through it, I could just see Samuel lying on the floor. The bed was in flames beside him. The flames were eight feet tall and licking the ceiling. All the furniture was on fire and the carpet on the floor was beginning to smolder. I took all this in in less than a second. I grabbed his ankles and pulled. He barely moved a couple of inches. I could feel my hands starting to blister in the heat. I knew in a few seconds, my clothes and the tea towels would dry and then burst into flames. I heaved again. I could see his hair was burning. I screwed up my eyes and heaved a third time, roaring like an insane thing, and now he moved and I was running backward as though his body had become weightless. Then I was crashing out of the room backward, gasping for air, and Dehan was shouting, "*Don't stop! Don't stop! Keep running!*"

But even as we dragged him down the hall, cops were grabbing his shoulders off the floor and we were bundling him out into the blessed cold and the rain. There I half dropped, half lowered him to the sidewalk and I staggered across the road, bent double, coughing violently and painfully. I took in the two fire trucks, the ambulance, and the backup patrol cars, and I took in Dehan, removing the wet tea towels from her head and her face.

"You are," she said, between coughs, "*the most* obstinate man in the world!"

I shook my head, wiping the rain from my face. "You shouldn't have done that."

"You're welcome!"

"I'm glad you did. Thanks."

"You'd be dead if I hadn't, you dumb son of a bitch!"

"I couldn't let him burn to death, Dehan. Is he alive?"

She shook her head. "I don't know." She jerked her chin toward the ambulance. Samuel was on a gurney with an oxygen mask over his face. We went over as he was being lifted into the ambulance. A red-haired paramedic glanced at me as we approached. I asked her, "Will he live?"

"Yeah. He has some nasty burns and he'll have a pretty bad hangover from the smoke. But he should be fine in a few days."

"How about his dad?"

She pointed her chin at the inside of the ambulance. He was sitting up with a blanket wrapped around his shoulders, watching his unconscious son being settled in beside him. He looked like he was in deep shock. I wiped my eyes and my mouth with the back of my sleeve and asked him, "Who's your doctor, Mr. Reynolds?"

He stared at me but didn't answer. The paramedic climbed in and grabbed the doors. "We have to get them to the hospital, Detective. We'll find his doctor."

I nodded. She pulled the doors closed and we watched the red rear lights disappear through the drizzle in the failing light of the late afternoon. I turned to Dehan. "You okay?"

She nodded. "You?"

"I want guards put on all their doors. Samuel's, the dad's, and Helen's. I don't want anybody—*anybody*—going in or out except their doctors and the nurses. I especially don't want them going into each other's rooms. Make sure they are separated. If anyone goes in, I want a cop to go in with them. Will you see to that?"

"Sure." She frowned.

I said, "You understand what I am saying. I want them kept away from each other."

"I get it, Stone. What are you going to do?"

"I need to have a word with Father Arundel. I won't be long."

What I learned from Father Arundel was exactly what I expected to learn. So I made a phone call to Blackstone's and joined Dehan ten minutes later, where she was sitting in the Jag, watching the fire department hose the house down while the cops evacuated the neighboring houses. I said, "Come on, let's go to the hospital and wrap this thing up."

She stared at me for a moment with mild surprise on her face, then went around and climbed in the passenger seat while I got behind the wheel. As we pulled away, with the growing flames playing on the wet road, Dehan was frowning. "I don't know how you plan to wrap it up, Stone. As far as I can see, we are exactly where we were. We can charge him with kidnapping, assault with a deadly weapon, and arson, but we still can't pin him to Celeste's murder."

I nodded. "That's true."

She eyed me awhile. "That's it? 'That's true.' That's your answer?"

"You're right. You deserve more. We'll play it by ear when we get there."

She looked away. "Dork."

"You know that was my nickname at school, right?"

"You told me."

Half an hour later, we arrived at the Jacobi and the receptionist, after looking dubiously at us and our badges, told us how to find the Reynoldses' rooms. They had put Samuel and his father next to each other, with a cop sitting outside each room. Helen was sleeping after surgery. The cut had not been life-threatening, but it had been deep and needed stitches. She was very traumatized and was under observation by a psychiatrist.

Samuel was awake. He had second-degree burns to his face and hands. When he saw us come in, he said, "I'll confess to everything and take my punishment."

I gave a single nod. "Don't you think we've had enough punishment and redemption and cleansing of sins for one night, Samuel? How about we stop burning things down and start building them up?"

He looked away at the black window, where distant lights and luminous raindrops speckled the glass. "I don't know what you mean."

I sat on the edge of a chair under that black window with my elbows on my knees and looked at his partially bandaged face.

"I'm not going to question you tonight, Samuel. You need to rest and sleep. We'll talk tomorrow. But I'd like you to think about something. Will you do that?"

"I never stop thinking." He said it sullenly, to the window.

"A lot of people got hurt tonight, a lot of innocent people. It's a miracle nobody got killed. Those people are paying the price for your guilt. Maybe it's time you started taking responsibility, instead of guilt-tripping everybody." His eyes shifted and he stared at me. I leaned over and patted his foot. "I'll see you tomorrow, not too early."

Out in the corridor, Dehan screwed up her face at me. "What was that supposed to mean, Stone? Take responsibility instead of guilt-tripping everybody. What does that mean?"

"It means it's time he took responsibility for what he's done."

She watched me go into the old man's room. He was sitting up in bed, looking depressed. A nurse was checking the bandages on the backs of his hands. I asked her, "How is he?" I showed her my badge. "Detective Stone. This is my partner, Detective Dehan."

She glanced at the badge and smiled at me. "He's fine. Some minor burns to his hands, but he'll be okay."

"Have you been able to locate his doctor?"

She frowned. "I'm not sure what you mean . . . Dr. Patel is just here . . ."

I nodded, then smiled. "Okay, thanks."

"Don't tire him. He needs rest."

She left us. Dehan sat on a chair on the far side of the bed, by the door. I sat on a chair under the window, where I had sat in his son's room.

"You're a very tough man, Mr. Reynolds. Good stock. Your whole family are as tough as old boot leather."

He gave something like a smile. "The Irish," he said. "We're a tough lot."

"Sure are. How's the angina?"

"I'll live."

"And the blood pressure? They must have checked that straightaway when you came in, right?"

He nodded. "It's under control."

"But you should give them your doctor's details, Sean, so they can contact him and get your medical records. That kind of thing is important."

"Oh yeah, I will, don't worry. They have everything under control."

"How long has it been?"

"What?"

"That you've been incapacitated by angina and high blood pressure?"

He shrugged. "Few years."

"You know, I don't know a lot about medicine, but I never heard of a case before where somebody was actually bedridden by high blood pressure and angina. I always thought gentle exercise was advisable. Just goes to show, right? What do I know?"

"Rest." He nodded several times. "That's the thing. Lots of rest, and don't get excited or upset."

"I asked Father Arundel."

"What?"

Dehan was frowning at me.

I said, "How long you had been bedridden. He said it was two years. He said it was your daughter's death that crippled you physically and emotionally."

He looked down at his hands on his lap. "I never did recover. Poor Samuel had to shoulder the burden of everything. He's a strong lad, but I suppose the pressure got to him, and he cracked."

"He supports all three of you, financially, doesn't he?"

"Him and a small pension from my wife's insurance. We get by."

"Because before, it was both of you working, wasn't it? You and Samuel both. Until Celeste was killed. Then you were broken by grief and he had to manage alone." He didn't answer. I waited a moment. Then I smiled and gave a small laugh. "Come on, Sean. It's over. And God knows, who could blame you? You did it for your family, didn't you? Nobody knows who hasn't been there on the front line, nobody can possibly know what it's like, trying to pull your family through, keeping them on the righteous path, on your own, with no help or support from anybody."

He looked back at his hands. "It's not easy."

"And when Celeste came along, she killed your wife, and in the same fell swoop drove poor Helen into a psychotic state. But you loved her nonetheless, right? God had taken your wife, but he had given you this beautiful little baby girl. Am I right?"

He nodded. "I adored her. I doted on her. I prayed every night and day that Helen would be healed, and I thanked the good Lord for giving me Samuel, he was my rock, my support. But most of all, I thanked the Lord for the love of my life, little Celeste. My child of heaven."

"It must have been tough when she strayed from the righteous path."

"I knew she would return. I knew she wouldn't stray far. I had faith that God would lead her back to me."

"But that weekend was more than any man could take. After all the love and devotion you had given her, after taking your wife and your eldest daughter from you, to then turn and insult you and heap abuse on you, to fall into sin and revel in it, be proud of it, boast about it, and finally, to cap it all, to tell you she was leaving—leaving to live in sin with a man. The ingratitude, the disloyalty to her own family, to her father. I get it, Sean. It must have been too much to bear."

He shook his head at his hands. He was silent for a long while. Then he said, "I don't know what you're talking about."

"Samuel tried to reason with her. She just gave him a mouthful of abuse. You interceded. Tried to calm them both, lead them back to the loving harmony of a Christian family. But she wouldn't have it and you ended up getting mad. Maybe you hoped, after she stormed up to her room, that she'd cool off and come to her senses and apologize. But instead of that, when she came down that evening, she gave you both more of the same."

He still wouldn't look at me, but he said, "That's old news."

"Sure, but I am willing to bet that that was when she dropped the bombshell that she'd been having an affair with Lenny. But now she was dumping him and moving in with Chad. And then you realized that what your son had been saying was true. She was evil, and her evil was spreading, touching not just her family now, but old friends too. Samuel called her and begged her to wait and talk. But instead of him, you went. You probably begged her to see sense, to return to the fold, but all she would do was scream at you."

He shook his head. "No. You're wrong."

"Was it the screaming, Sean? Was it the screaming that made you snap and want to shut her up? And before you realized what you'd done, she was dead. You repented and put your arms around her. Chad saw you, standing there, hugging her. You picked her up, put her in the truck, and took her to Blackstone's. You broke in—you knew there was no alarm on the gate and no CCTV. You dragged her through the improvised gate in the fence, loaded her down with rubble, and dropped her in the river."

He shook his head again, small shakes, still staring at his hands. "I don't know. I don't know what you're on about."

"At first, we were thrown by your being bedridden. You looked so frail. But that isn't a physical condition at all, is it? It's emotional. You're an emotional wreck, but physically you are an ox, just like your son. Your angina and your blood pressure, it's all self-diagnosed, isn't it? You haven't even got a doctor. And when I realized that, I realized it wasn't Sam Reynolds that worked at Blackstone's, it was Sean."

"I'm ill, I need you to go now. I need to rest. All this, it'll bring on my angina and my blood pressure."

I stood and went to the door. I poked my head out and asked the uniform sitting there. "Have they arrived?"

He glanced down the passage a bit. I followed his gaze, smiled, and said, "Please come in."

Geoff and Kate Blackstone approached and stepped into the room. Geoff beamed. "Reynolds! What have you been up to, you old dog? What is this all about?"

Sean covered his face with his hands and started to weep. Kate frowned at me. I said, "It wasn't Sam, was it? It was Sean."

"If you'd asked me from the start, I would have told you. Geoff has no memory at all, but I remember everything. Sean Reynolds. That's him." She gave me a lurid smile. "What has he done?"

I sighed. "He's been cheating the Devil."

EPILOGUE

It was still raining. It looked as though it would never stop. Occasionally, a human body transited across the window, wrapped in a mac or an anorak, leaning slightly forward, pushing an umbrella into the wind. I didn't care. Nothing could touch me.

I was lying on the sofa, watching the trees bow and toss, watching the desultory passersby getting wet. I had been propped with pillows under my neck and under my socked feet, and I had a large glass of Bushmills balanced on my belly. In my nostrils, I had the delicious blend of roasting lamb tinged with woodsmoke from where Dehan was hunkered down, lighting the fire. I heard it crackle and spark, and then she came over, lifted my feet, and sat under them, resting them down on her lap as she picked up her martini.

"Level with me, when did you first suspect Sean?"

"Day one."

"Come on!"

"That was when the first alarm bells went off. He was too much, too devoted, too committed to his family, too devout in his religion, and yet . . ." I shook my head. "He wasn't really any of those things. What he was under that patriarchal exterior was a lazy narcissist who was not devoted to his family at all, but wanted his family devoted to him.

"Then I started to be more suspicious when we told them about Lenny. I never really bought Lenny as Celeste's killer. The circumstantial evidence against him was strong, but it all pointed to the affair, not to his killing her, and the disposal of the body pointed firmly to an amateur, not a pro like Lenny. And when we gave Sean and Samuel the news, Sean stated categorically that Lenny did not kill his Celeste. Samuel was shocked, incensed, outraged, furious, but Sean simply repeated over and over that Lenny had not killed her. He didn't say he couldn't have, he said he *didn't*. He was categorical. That told me that he knew who *had* killed her.

"His physical condition seemed to rule him out, but it was always in the back of my mind that it could be psychosomatic, or simply that he was a lazy bastard who felt sorry for himself and wanted the world waiting on him.

"Then, when Samuel wanted me to cleanse Helen's soul and rid her of Celeste's evil, it struck me very forcefully that he could not do it himself. He was incapable. He wanted me to take the responsibility for the killing. That was not congruent with his having killed Celeste with his own bare hands.

"And the clincher was when I tried to drag him out of the bed and I saw how damned big and strong he was. He was not the frail old man he liked to pretend to be. He was an ox, at least as strong as his son, and he fit Chad's description just as well or better.

"So I asked Father Arundel how long he had been bedridden —we had assumed for some reason that it had been for a long time—but it had only been *since* his daughter's death. So at the time of her death, he was just as able-bodied as anybody else, and he had just as much motive, or more. So I called Geoff Blackstone and asked him to ask his wife what Reynolds' first name was. She came back straightaway: not Sam, but Sean. Remember, we told Geoff it was Sam Reynolds. He agreed—it's an easy mistake to make. But his wife was the one with the excellent memory, and she remembered it was Sean, not Sam. So I asked them to come over to the hospital to identify him."

She sat gazing at the fire, nodding slowly with her bottom lip stuck out. "It never crossed my mind."

"I won't say he was my number one suspect, but I just had this constant nagging feeling, all the other suspects just didn't quite fit."

We sat in comfortable, companionable silence for a while, sipping our drinks and listening to the fire crackle and occasionally spit. Dehan's gaze was lost in the flames, with the orange light tinting her skin. After a while, she said, "Stone, I don't want kids." She looked at me and I frowned. "I'm focused on my career. But, you know, if we did, eventually, one day, decide to have kids, and build that extension, what do you think it would be, a boy or a girl?"

"I really don't mind."

"But what do you think?"

"Well, it might be a boy, or it might be a girl."

"If it was a boy, what would we call him?"

"I always liked Thorvald, or maybe Bullvine . . ."

"Be serious . . ."

"Perhaps Ragnar . . ."

"Stone!"

Don't miss TRICK OR TREAT. The riveting sequel in the Dead Cold Mystery series.

Scan the QR code below to purchase TRICK OR TREAT.

Or go to: righthouse.com/trick-or-treat

NOTE: flip to the very end to read an exclusive sneak peak...

DON'T MISS ANYTHING!

If you want to stay up to date on all new releases in this series, with this author, or with any of our new deals, you can do so by joining our newsletters below.

In addition, you will immediately gain access to our entire *Right House VIP Library,* which includes many riveting Mystery and Thriller novels for your enjoyment!

righthouse.com/email

(Easy to unsubscribe. No spam. Ever.)

ALSO BY BLAKE BANNER

Up to date books can be found at:
www.righthouse.com/blake-banner

ROGUE THRILLERS
Gates of Hell (Book 1)
Hell's Fury (Book 2)

ALEX MASON THRILLERS
Odin (Book 1)
Ice Cold Spy (Book 2)
Mason's Law (Book 3)
Assets and Liabilities (Book 4)
Russian Roulette (Book 5)
Executive Order (Book 6)
Dead Man Talking (Book 7)
All The King's Men (Book 8)
Flashpoint (Book 9)
Brotherhood of the Goat (Book 10)
Dead Hot (Book 11)
Blood on Megiddo (Book 12)
Son of Hell (Book 13)

HARRY BAUER THRILLER SERIES
Dead of Night (Book 1)
Dying Breath (Book 2)
The Einstaat Brief (Book 3)
Quantum Kill (Book 4)
Immortal Hate (Book 5)
The Silent Blade (Book 6)
LA: Wild Justice (Book 7)

Breath of Hell (Book 8)
Invisible Evil (Book 9)
The Shadow of Ukupacha (Book 10)
Sweet Razor Cut (Book 11)
Blood of the Innocent (Book 12)
Blood on Balthazar (Book 13)
Simple Kill (Book 14)
Riding The Devil (Book 15)
The Unavenged (Book 16)
The Devil's Vengeance (Book 17)
Bloody Retribution (Book 18)
Rogue Kill (Book 19)
Blood for Blood (Book 20)

DEAD COLD MYSTERY SERIES
An Ace and a Pair (Book 1)
Two Bare Arms (Book 2)
Garden of the Damned (Book 3)
Let Us Prey (Book 4)
The Sins of the Father (Book 5)
Strange and Sinister Path (Book 6)
The Heart to Kill (Book 7)
Unnatural Murder (Book 8)
Fire from Heaven (Book 9)
To Kill Upon A Kiss (Book 10)
Murder Most Scottish (Book 11)
The Butcher of Whitechapel (Book 12)
Little Dead Riding Hood (Book 13)
Trick or Treat (Book 14)
Blood Into Wine (Book 15)
Jack In The Box (Book 16)
The Fall Moon (Book 17)
Blood In Babylon (Book 18)
Death In Dexter (Book 19)
Mustang Sally (Book 20)

A Christmas Killing (Book 21)
Mommy's Little Killer (Book 22)
Bleed Out (Book 23)
Dead and Buried (Book 24)
In Hot Blood (Book 25)
Fallen Angels (Book 26)
Knife Edge (Book 27)
Along Came A Spider (Book 28)
Cold Blood (Book 29)
Curtain Call (Book 30)

THE OMEGA SERIES
Dawn of the Hunter (Book 1)
Double Edged Blade (Book 2)
The Storm (Book 3)
The Hand of War (Book 4)
A Harvest of Blood (Book 5)
To Rule in Hell (Book 6)
Kill: One (Book 7)
Powder Burn (Book 8)
Kill: Two (Book 9)
Unleashed (Book 10)
The Omicron Kill (Book 11)
9mm Justice (Book 12)
Kill: Four (Book 13)
Death In Freedom (Book 14)
Endgame (Book 15)

ABOUT US

Right House is an independent publisher created by authors for readers. We specialize in Action, Thriller, Mystery, and Crime novels.

If you enjoyed this novel, then there is a good chance you will like what else we have to offer! Please stay up to date by using any of the links below.

Join our mailing lists to stay up to date -->
righthouse.com/email
Visit our website --> righthouse.com
Contact us --> contact@righthouse.com

 facebook.com/righthousebooks
 x.com/righthousebooks
 instagram.com/righthousebooks

EXCLUSIVE SNEAK PEAK OF...

TRICK OR TREAT

CHAPTER 1

I was looking through the window at the ash-gray sky. The naked plane trees looked cold, and the occasional, drifting flakes of sleet made them look colder. The search for cold cases on a day like this seemed almost an unwarranted excess. Desultory cars, their headlamps switched on despite it being only eleven a.m., sighed on the wet blacktop. People, muffled like Eskimos, leaned forward as they walked, with their hands deep in their pockets.

It was December. It was December with a vengeance.

Dehan was not looking out the window. She was chewing the butt end of a pencil and frowning at the insides of an old manila file.

"This case," she said without looking up, "was twelve years old last Halloween. We should have a look at it."

I examined the content of my mug and found there was nothing. It was empty but for the dregs. "Why, because it just had its birthday?"

"Cosmic cycles." She looked up, ignoring my bitter humor, and frowned a little harder. "Cosmic cycles," she said again. "Twelve months in the year, twelve signs in the zodiac . . . And also it seems insoluble. Not locked-room insoluble—that's always a hidden hole in the wall—but a genuine puzzle."

I reached out my hand and she tossed over the file. As I leafed through it, she started to recite.

"Sue Benedict, twenty-four, died on Halloween, three days before her twenty-fifth birthday. Sucks, huh?"

"Born in November," I said, scanning the ME's report. "All the best people are."

"Yeah, right. So, her body was found in the bedroom, on the bed, raped, strangled, and stabbed."

"How do we know she was raped and not just killed post-coitus?"

"Abrasions on her inner thighs and around her groin suggest she fought against him. Also, there was a lot of premortem bruising on her neck and thighs, suggesting there was a sexual struggle before he killed her.

"The position of the body on the bed, with the legs spread open, and the bruising from the thumbs on the trachea, suggest that strangulation occurred either during or immediately at the end of the actual rape, while he was still on top of her. He then followed up with what looks like a frenzy of stabbing in the belly, especially around the lower belly. Apparently this is consistent with sexual rage, as it mimics the act of penetration. Semen was fresh and they were able to get a profile. He also left clear finger and thumbprints all over her body, especially her neck and throat. No match was found on CODIS or IAFIS. Swabs and prints were taken from everyone at the party, but no match was found there either."

I put the file down and considered her across the desk, lacing my fingers over my belly. "Suggestive of somebody who knew her, wanted her, but was rejected."

She nodded, then shrugged. The whole thing was a "yeah, maybe" in body language. "It could also suggest a stalker who had been building up a fantasy at a distance. More suggestive is the fact that her windows were all locked from the inside and the door had not been forced. So either her attacker had somehow got hold of a key, or she let him in."

"She had been at a Halloween party..."

"Yup. Seems she was involved in some art group based at the Bethlehem Church hall, near the corner of Lacombe and Thieriot. Had nothing to do with the church, they just rented the hall three nights a week."

I managed to frown and raise my eyebrows in a complicated expression of skeptical surprise. "That's a lot of dedication to art. Usually it's just once a week, isn't it?"

"I wouldn't know, Sensei. Anyhow, this group must have been pretty tight, because they arranged a Halloween party at one of their houses. I think the house belonged to the guy who led the group. On..."

She screwed up her forehead, trying to remember, and I said, "Taylor Avenue, within staggering distance of Sue's house..."

"... On the corner of Patterson. Seems she left the party at about two a.m. A neighbor raised the alarm the next morning. He had seen comings and goings at the house the night before, and when he got up for breakfast, he saw her door was still open."

I sighed. "Art, sex, and a murder, all at Halloween. Edgar Allan Poe meets Georges Simenon. Did you know, Dehan, that turpentine is an aphrodisiac?"

"No, Stone, I didn't know that."

"Yup, that is why you rarely see nudes draped languidly across the beds of writers, but you will often see them in that attitude across the beds of painters."

"Huh. How about musicians?"

"That depends on the style of music, Dehan. Composers and performers in Tudor, Renaissance, Baroque, and classical you will very rarely find with nudes across their beds. However, rock and roll is notoriously sexual."

"Sex, drugs, and rock and roll."

I wagged my pen at her. "In the words of the mighty Dylan, 'Lay across my big brass bed.'"

"Lay across my big brass bed?"

"That is what he said. So what do you say we go and have a look at this church hall and talk to whoever was in charge at the time; see what they can tell us about this bunch of wild, wayward Bohemians?"

She stood. "I say, lead me to the turpentine, Sensei."

It was extremely cold outside. Shards of icy air stabbed through whatever small opening they could find in your clothes and froze small patches of your skin, making your whole body shiver. I looked at Dehan as she stamped across the road toward my Jaguar, with her cheeks flushed pink under a brown woolen hat pulled low over her ears. She was also clapping her gloved hands as she stamped.

We clambered into the car (a burgundy 1964 Mark II, which I had brought with me from England years back) billowing clouds of condensation, slammed the doors, and I turned the key in the ignition. The big, old engine growled and I reversed out of the lot.

It was less than a mile down Soundview Avenue to the Bethlehem Church. As we turned right out of Story, Dehan said, "You know where the mystery lies for me, Stone?"

I glanced at her.

She went on. "The guy knows her. She knows him. That's why she let him in. That's how they come to be in her bedroom with no signs of a struggle. But he makes no effort to hide his DNA. He goes right ahead and rapes her and strangles her. Makes no effort to hide his identity at all. It's like he is super confident that no match is going to be found."

I nodded a lot, chewing my lip. "That is very interesting, Dehan. I agree. It could be the key to the answer."

"And then, he just vanishes. Nobody has seen him, nobody has any idea who he is. He's like . . ."

"Please don't say a ghost. I know it's thematic, with the whole Halloween thing, but don't."

She tried to arch an eyebrow at me, but her woolen hat

wouldn't let her. "I wasn't going to . . . I was going to say a ghoul."

I turned into Thieriot Avenue and pulled up outside a large, white church that looked as though it might have been more at home in a Mexican desert. It was chunky and square in design. The walls were lime washed and there was a giant, wooden cross on the roof above the door. Beyond an iron fence and gate, steps that had been painted oxblood red climbed to an arched wooden door in which two crosses had been cut. To the side of the building there was a large lawn, and at the back I could see a long, low clapboard building, which I guessed was the hall.

The church door stood slightly ajar, like God knew we were coming but didn't want anybody else disturbing his Monday morning with a pot of coffee and the *New York Times*. We clambered out of the car and, as I locked it, Dehan jumped up and down for a bit, billowed vapor from her mouth like a small, woolen dragon, and stamped up the steps to the door. I followed.

Inside, it was dark. Only the golden altar at the far end, beyond the transept, was illuminated. There, candles wavered and reflected off the crucifix, the gilt on the walls, and the frames of the paintings.

We proceeded down the central aisle. I coughed and it ricocheted around the rafters on the ceiling, knocking against the echoes of our footsteps. Out of the shadows beyond the transept, a small man with big eyebrows appeared, as though he'd been dislodged by my cough. He was little more than five feet tall, with a bald, shiny head, brown corduroy trousers, and a sage-green cardigan. He was holding a cloth and a can of furniture wax. The smell was both strong and oddly reassuring.

He looked at us uncertainly, in turn, one after the other, suggesting he was uncertain about both of us. Dehan said, "Are you the guy who takes care of things around here?"

His shoulders rose slowly and his head tilted to one side, like he was shrugging in tai chi. Then he spread his hands: shrugging tiger, uncertain dragon.

"I am not the padre. I am only the handyman." His accent was more Spanish than Hispanic.

I showed him my badge. "I'm Detective Stone, this is Detective Dehan. We're with the NYPD. What's your name?"

"I am Juan de la Torre."

"How long have you worked here, Juan?"

"Twenty, almost twenty-five years. I am naturalize now. I come from Spain . . ." He said "Espaing," but I knew what he meant.

"Do you remember a group of artists who used to rent the church hall, about twelve years ago?"

He nodded. "They still rentin' it. Mr. Giorgio Gonzalez, he is teachin' his classes there, couple of nights por week."

Dehan asked him, "Do you remember the group back then, one Halloween . . . ?"

He was nodding before she had finished. "And the nice woman, Sue, she was kill. I remember. It make me very sad." He pointed back past the transept. "You wanna come in my room? I make some coffee an' you can ask me. Is very cold here in the nave."

We followed him past the altar into the shadows. He pushed open an arched wooden door and led us into a small, neat room with a bed, a small cooker, a table, and four chairs. There was also a single armchair in front of an iron wood burner, and beside it a small bookcase with a couple of dozen books. None of them was the Bible. He saw Dehan reading the spines and sighed.

"I am a communist and an atheist. I told Padre Romero, but he say he don't care. He is a communist and an atheist also. Sometimes he invite me to eat in his house. He is a good man. From Puerto Rico. Please, sit. You like some coffee?"

We sat at the old wooden table and he poured us black coffee. He put a carton of milk on the table and a dish of sugar. We all sipped and he said, "I remember this group. Giorgio Gonzalez is the teacher, back then also. He is Mexican. All the women like him because he has the strong personality, lots of temperament." He gave a small laugh. "I think maybe it is a bit of theater, you know? But he is not a bad artist." He leaned toward Dehan and narrowed his eyes. "Perhaps he is a little bit prisoner of his own culture. You understand what I am saying. He paints like a Mexican in New York. Picasso, Monet, Van Gogh, Goya, they are painting like human beings in the world. Their art is for the everybody. But Giorgio is painting like a Mexican, so he is painting for himself. Is just my opinion."

I smiled. "That is a very good observation. So you said you remember Sue?"

"Yes, of course. She was a nice girl." His face lit up. "Always laughing. Always with a big smile on her face. I like her, and she is always happy to talk. Many people are thinking, 'Oh, Juan is the cleaner. It is no good people see me talking with him.' But no Sue. Sue was off the people. Nice girl."

Dehan asked him, "Can you remember anything that happened around that time that was unusual, that struck you as strange in the behavior of the group?"

He made a face, pulled his mouth down at the corners, and shook his head. "No, the detective ask me the same thing. Nothing . . ." He shrugged again. "Nothing, everything normal, they come in for their lessons, they always laughin', he is teachin' them, makin' a bit of theater, 'Hey, look at me, I am an artist' . . . I remember she was kill on Tuesday. On Monday they have a class and it is a nude girl. Giorgio was jokin' with Sue if she want to be the model. But she say no, and they get a model to come and pose. Pretty girl, nice figure, but *she* was complainin' about the cold. Giorgio was laughin' at her, flirtin', comin' on to her. In the end, I have to go get some more heaters for her because she said otherwise she was leavin'." He looked down at his coffee with a sad face, like coffee just wasn't coffee anymore. "Pretty girl," he said. "Giorgio no respect her."

"Nothing else remarkable happened? Nobody new joined the group? Sue didn't seem different in any way . . . ?"

He shook his head. "No, no, nothin' like that. Everything was normal."

I said, "Who were the people she was closest to, Juan?"

Now he smiled at his coffee. It was a lopsided smile, and after a moment, he looked up and met my eye, then Dehan's. "She like Giorgio. A lot. She use to tell me, 'Oh, Juan, I am crazy about Giorgio! But he don't see me at all! Is like I am no here!'" He laughed. "She really upset when Giorgio was comin' on to the model. I tell her, 'No! You are wrong! He like you, but he playing hard to get. You should be cool with him!' But she don't listen. Until . . ." He paused for dramatic effect. "Fernando join the group."

"Who is Fernando?"

"Fernando Martinez. He is an ol' friend of Giorgio. He is also from Mexico. Women also like him. He is good artist, better than Giorgio in my opinion. So when he is joining the group, Sue is not knowing which way she wanna go: to Giorgio who is ignoring her, or to Fernando who is comin' on strong?"

I laughed. "So what happened?"

He spread his hands, shrugged, and nodded in a way that could only be Mediterranean. "Immediately this happen, Giorgio is all over Sue, and Giorgio and Fernando are competin' with each other for her attention. It was the stupidest thing I ever seen in my life. They was like fifteen-year-old teenagers, you know?"

Dehan drained her cup and set it down on the table, frowning to herself. "When did this happen? How long before she was killed?"

"Oh, very short time, I think like the month before, or two months. I think about it many times because it was sad. He only realize he have to fight for her, when it was too late."

I examined the dregs of black liquid in my own cup for a moment and asked, without looking up, "Juan, did you ever form an opinion about who might have killed Sue?"

He made a long "pfff . . ." noise. "My opinion is only my opinion. You cannot send a man to prison because of my opinion.

But, you know this because you are cops, so this is my *opinion*! People kill for money and sex. I don't know about any money problems with Sue. Maybe she have them, I am not saying she didn't have money problems with somebody! I don't know. I just saying I didn't know about any. But . . ." He nodded a lot, using his whole body. "I *do* know about sex problem, with Fernando and Giorgio. Mexicans, like Spanish, are very jealous people. The night she is kill, she is at a Halloween party with Fernando and Giorgio . . ." He held up his hands like somebody was pointing a gun at him. "You can take out your own conclusions from this. I don't wanna say nothin'. But sometimes, when two men are real close, an' a woman is come between them, they can punish the woman, instead of kill each other."

"Point taken. Was there anybody else close to her at that time that you noticed?"

"Not that I can remember. Better you ask Giorgio. He still livin' here, still doin' the classes."

I looked at Dehan. She shook her head and turned to Juan.

"Thank you, Juan, you have been very helpful. Stay here in the warm, we'll see ourselves out."

As we stood, he watched us a moment. "You openin' the cold case, huh? I hope you get him. She was nice girl."

Dehan nodded. "We'll get him. Don't you worry."

We let ourselves out and closed the door behind us, then crossed the long, dark nave toward the gray, icy day outside.

CHAPTER 2

It was walking distance, but with the wind picking up and whipping sleet and tiny shards of ice off the East River, and burying them in our skin like frozen shrapnel, we got in the Jag and drove the two hundred yards to Patterson Avenue. Two right turns and another hundred and fifty yards saw us parked outside something that looked like a giant boathouse. It was tall—four stories tall—and narrow: not more than twenty-five feet across. Like many of the houses in that area, it was clapboard, with a long, sloping, gabled roof and tall, narrow windows on the upper floors. There was a garage facing the street on the first floor, and a flight of ten stone steps led up to a kind of veranda at the side of the house and what looked like the front door.

Dehan led the way, still stamping and clapping her hands, picked a path through half-carved hunks of tree, and rang on the bell beside the blue door. It was opened after a couple of minutes by a man in his late forties. What had once been thick, curly black hair was now going gray and thinning on top. He had large brown eyes, a heavy moustache, and gray stubble on his cheeks. He gazed at Dehan a moment like he was thinking there might be an attractive woman underneath all those clothes. Then he gave me a careful once-over, like he was wondering if I would stop him from removing all those clothes. My face and my badge said I would.

"Mr. Gonzalez? Giorgio Gonzalez?"

"Yeah, that's me. Why?"

There was a trace of an accent. I told him who we were, then added, "We'd like to ask you some questions about Sue Benedict. May we come in?"

He sighed. "Sue?" He looked Dehan over a couple of times and stepped back. "Yeah, why not? Come on in."

We stepped over the threshold and directly into a large space with wooden floors and a high ceiling. A fire was burning in a huge, six-foot square fireplace with a bare-brick chimney breast. There were rugs and skins strewn across the floor, heavy linen chairs and a sofa were scattered with careful abandon around the fire, and at the far end of the room there was a massive, wooden table that seemed to be handmade out of raw hunks of tree. Each of the six chairs around it was different, but carefully so. Everywhere there were paintings—some on the walls, others stacked against the walls in reams of five and six—and everywhere there was the smell of turpentine. A giant easel stood near the fireplace, with a large semiabstract nude on it. I stood and looked at it for a moment, thinking how far we had come from Picasso. To him an abstract was an abstraction of form. This was just an ugly distortion of it.

I turned my attention to Giorgio. He was wearing jeans and a T-shirt, and I noticed he was barefoot. Looking at him made me feel cold, but I realized the room was very warm.

He gestured at us, and there was mockery in his eyes, a mockery I figured was habitual. "You can take off your coats. I got triple glazing, and the fire makes a lot of heat, you know?"

He fell onto the sofa, with his arms thrown carelessly along the back, and watched us sit, unbuttoning our coats. His expression seemed to suggest that he was both wise and liberated, and that we drones of the "Establishment" were endemically stupid and did stupid things, like wearing coats in warm rooms. He looked at Dehan as she dragged off her hat.

"You should wear your hair down, *guajira*, it suits the shape of your face, and your neck."

She sighed. "Gee, thanks, Sancho."

A spasm of irritation crossed his face. "What do you want to know about Sue? It was a long time ago."

Dehan spoke, looking at her hat. "How close were you two?"

"You mean was I fuckin' her?"

She frowned hard, still looking at her woolen hat, then placed it on her lap and turned to him. "Is that what I asked you?"

He spread out his arms and crossed his bare ankles, smiling at how stupid the whole damn world was. "I'm just asking. You know, people are usually so scared to talk about sex. They use this crazy euphemisms..."

"What did I ask you?"

"Sure, but I thought maybe..."

"I asked you how close you were. You want to answer the question instead of offering me half-assed theories about social repression? Would that be okay?"

"Woah!" He held up his hands. "Hostile, baby!"

I sighed. My stomach was telling me it was lunchtime and this guy was standing between me and lunch. I said, "Mr. Gonzalez, would you mind answering the question, please? The question was very clear. It doesn't need interpreting. How close were you to Sue Benedict?"

"My apologies, man. Just trying to be clear. She was my private student. I think at one time she maybe had a thing for me. A lot of my students do. We became friends. That was about it."

"What about in the rest of the group? Was there anyone else she was close to?"

His face was a perfect blank, like the question didn't mean anything to him. He gave his head a small shake. "I don't know."

Dehan said, "You met three times a week?"

"Yeah."

"That's a lot of dedication on their part."

"What can I tell you? I'm a good teacher, there was a nice feeling in the class, we had a good groove, you know what I'm saying? We'd put on some music, have a little wine, and paint, man. Paint the night away!"

He laughed and Dehan smiled. "So you had a good rapport with your students. Did they confide in you, discuss their feelings with you? Was it that kind of thing?"

He gave a lopsided smile which you got the feeling he'd practiced a lot in front of the mirror. "Hey, babe, I am just a private art teacher, you know what I'm telling you? You gonna hear some lost souls out there say I got a lot of natural wisdom and insight into people's souls. I did my peyote back home with the shaman, I seen my eagle, but I am just a regular guy who knows how to paint. Maybe..."

I sighed loudly. "Mr. Gonzalez, you're preaching to the choir. I believe you. You convinced me. You are just an ordinary guy, and if I need philosophy, I will go to John Locke or David Hume. Believe me, I won't come to you. We are not asking for insights into anybody's soul. All we want to know is whether Sue had any close relationships in the group, or if anybody was trying to get close to her."

He watched me a moment, shaking his head. "Hey, man, you guys are real hostile, you know that? I invited you into my home, and you're coming at me with this shit."

Dehan stared down at her boots. "Is there any reason, Mr. Gonzalez, why you don't want to answer this very simple question? Did Sue have any close relationships within the group?"

"No." He shook his head and was beginning to look mad. "No reason, and no close relationships."

"What about with Fernando?"

His eyebrows shot up. "Fernando?" He shrugged. "They fooled around a bit, you know what I mean? She liked to flirt, liked to play around, but she was never serious about Fernando. Fernando is a *pendejo*. I love that guy, but you can never take him seriously. He's a player, always on the surface, playing games. He never goes deep, you feel me?"

The question was directed at Dehan, with what he probably thought were smoldering eyes.

I asked, "So there was no rivalry between you and Fernando for Sue's affection?"

He threw his head back, with his arms along the back of the sofa, and laughed out loud. It was too loud and went on too long, so it became almost embarrassing. After a moment, Dehan looked at me and gave her head a small shake. She said quietly, "I was thinking tonight maybe a moussaka? It's so cold..."

I nodded. "Yeah, maybe some prawns and avocado to start, and we could pick up some wine..."

Giorgio stopped laughing but kept a trace of amused irony on his lips. "I'm sorry," he said. "Sometimes the absurdity of people, you know...? People don't understand how I feel..."

Dehan said to me, "Yeah, that sounds good..."

We both turned to look at him. I asked, "You done? So I take it there was no rivalry between you and Fernando..."

He chuckled and shook his head, then affected to make a serious face while winking at Dehan. "No, Detective Stone, there was no rivalry between me and Fernando."

Dehan leaned forward with her elbows on her knees. "Were you aware of anybody in the group who might have had strong feelings for Sue?"

He seemed to think for a while, gazing up at his walls. A couple of times he seemed about to shrug and finally said, "When you say group..."

Dehan flopped back in her chair. I let out a sigh that was on its way to becoming a groan. "It's not complicated, Mr. Gonzalez. Your group of students, or indeed anybody else. Can you think of anybody, either among your students or elsewhere, who might have had strong feelings about Sue?"

He managed to look vaguely pained. "You know, Detective, when I am with my students I am thinking about..." He paused, searching for words, with his hands held up like he was making an offering. "Texture . . . light . . . balance . . ." He gave me a pitying look. "I am not thinking about village gossip, who is fucking who, who has a crush on who . . ."

Dehan sat forward, her face flushed red, but I beat her to it. I said, "Texture? You are interested in texture? Have you ever seen the texture of a tongue when somebody has been strangled? It's like a sponge. And color? The color is a dark blueberry, but it starts to turn to gray after a while. And the face has a weird texture too, like somebody has used a bicycle pump to fill it with water. Kind of bloated and also spongy. Would you like to see the pictures of your friend Sue, after she was strangled, the texture, the color, the balance?"

I sat forward and spoke quietly. "Now, I advise you to listen very carefully to me, Giorgio, because this could make an important difference to your life. Sue Benedict was raped. While she was being raped, she was being threatened with death and possibly mutilation. She must have been terrified out of her mind. Are you capable of imagining what that felt like? After she was raped, the son of a bitch who did it to her then strangled her, and she suffered the most horrific death a person can experience, by suffocation. This bastard then took a knife and went into a frenzy of stabbing all over her belly. Is that enough texture and color for you?"

I paused, examining his face, then went on. "Now, I can see that you don't give a rat's ass about anything that isn't about you. That's fine. But next time I ask you a question, or my partner asks you a question, you are going to give a clear, concise, civil answer. Because if you don't, I am going to drag your sorry ass down to the station house and charge you with obstruction of justice, conspiracy to commit murder, and possession of marijuana and cocaine. You will do time. Have I made myself clear to you?"

At the last couple of sentences, his face had gone a pasty gray and he raised his hands as though I was pointing a gun at him. "Okay, man, it ain't necessary to . . ."

"Don't start."

He closed his mouth and swallowed.

"Do you know of anybody who had strong feelings for Sue, yes or no?"

"No. Fernando liked her, but it was cool. What I am trying to tell you is that, maybe there were things going on in the class and I just didn't notice."

I nodded. "No kidding. Try putting down that mirror sometimes, you might get to see what goes on around you. Can you give us a list of the students you had at that time?"

"Is twelve years ago, man."

"Yes or no?"

He shook his head. "No, I can remember a few people, but not all of them." Then he frowned. "But, you know what? I gave a list to the detective at the time. You gotta have it in your file, right?"

Dehan asked him, "What happened that night? At the party?"

He groaned and rubbed his face with his hands. I noticed they were strong hands and his forearms were corded with hard muscles. He took his hands away from his face and there was an expression of helplessness there. "What happened at the party? What happens at parties. People drink. People dance. We played salsa, rumba, maybe some people smoked dope—not me, I never smoke marijuana!" He laughed. "Sue was tripping . . ."

I frowned. "On acid?"

"No, man, on the vibe, a natural high. She was dancin', flirting, driving all the guys crazy. She was nice-lookin', you know? Nice body. She was dancin' a lot with Fernando. Then she was givin' me a lap dance!" He laughed a lot. "Sometimes it seems like yesterday. I thought she was gonna stay the night. And Fernando, poor son of a bitch, he was thinkin' he was gonna go home with her and she was gonna fuck with him. But then she told me she ain't feeling so good and she's gonna go home. She tells me maybe I can go over later and wake her up." He made an ugly face and shrugged. "There are plenty of babes at the party, you feel me? I don't need to go chasin' after Sue. I can get fucked right here in my own house. I told her to go to hell and that night I stay with . . ." He gazed up at the ceiling. "Rocio . . . Karen, Karen was from Sweden, and Ruby. They were nice kids." He made an expression that might have been regret. "Next day the pigs . . . sorry, the cops, come around tellin' me Sue is dead. So that's what happened that night."

Dehan thought for a minute. "Any idea where we can find Fernando?"

"Yeah, man. We still hang out. I've known that *pendejo* all my life. He's got an apartment in that cute house above the liquor store, by the public library, on Soundview." He held his hands in front of his face as though he was turning dials. "It's all decorated with zigzag white bricks. I like that house. It's cool."

There was a chime then from the front doorbell. Giorgio hesitated a moment, then stood. As he made his way to the door, I looked at Dehan. She shrugged and said, "I think we're wasting our time. I have no more questions."

I looked up at the ceiling, at the walls, and at the huge fireplace, then at all the paintings. I heard a woman's voice coming from the door.

"I hope I am not interrupting anything. I just made a huge meat casserole, far too much for me, and I thought you might like some . . ."

"Oh, Sandy, that is so generous. You have such a warm soul . . ."

I stood, and Dehan stood with me. They were both looking at us, Giorgio with hostile eyes, the woman with curiosity. She was a youthful forty with a pretty face and a slim, shapely figure which you could see because she had unbuttoned her coat. Her clothes were in stark contrast to Giorgio's: a high-necked blouse with a frill, a string of pearls, a dark skirt, stockings, and high-heeled shoes. Her hair was blond and taken up in a neat bun. She smiled at us.

"I was just saying to Giorgio that I hope I am not interrupting. I tend to cook far too much for myself, and I just *know* that he doesn't look after *him*self! These creative, artistic souls!" She laughed.

I said, "Don't worry, we were just leaving. Are you a neighbor?"

"Sure. I live just across the road!"

"How long have you lived here, Miss . . . ?"

"Beach, Sandy Beach! Can you believe it?" She laughed again, then held Giorgio's arm with the hand that wasn't holding the casserole. "Well, now, let me see. It must be about eight or nine years, or thereabouts."

I nodded and smiled, then turned to Giorgio. "It's narcissistic, your work. Too self-involved. Try looking outward. Enjoy your casserole."

We stepped out into the cold and heard the door close behind us. As we went down the steps, shivering with the icy wind, I felt unreasonably angry. As I unlocked the car, Dehan leaned on the roof and squinted at me.

"Before we go see Fernando, I need some lunch. That asshole made me angry and hungry."

I nodded. "Agreed."

CHAPTER 3

WE PICKED UP A COUPLE OF BURGERS AND SOME FRIES and sat in the car eating in silence and looking at the freezing world outside. Everybody was either leaning into the wind or hunched away from it. Everybody was padded and had their shoulders up by their ears, and everybody was wearing woolen hats. I said:

"Fernando is just going to tell us the same as Giorgio. Either because it's true, or because he phoned him as soon as we left and told him we were on our way."

Dehan looked at me, a little surprised, and taking small bites of a fry with her front teeth.

"So . . . ?"

"I don't want to go and see Fernando. I want to go and see Rafa Montilla, the detective who had the case to begin with."

"Why?" She shoved the rest of the fry in her mouth with her finger.

"This case isn't just cold, Dehan. It's arctic, like this damn weather. What have we got in the way of witnesses? We have two wiseass artists who wouldn't notice a performing elephant in the room unless it had a photograph of them pasted onto it, and the handyman at the church. Three very limited, very subjective perspectives. We need something broader and more detached to help us choose a line of inquiry."

She nodded into her greasy paper cone. "Okay, makes sense."

While I finished my burger, she called the precinct, got Rafa's number, and arranged to meet him at the Britches Sports Bar on Miles Avenue, in Throggs Neck. It was a ten-minute drive that took almost twenty because I was driving slowly, turning something over and over in my mind. Finally, as we were approaching the bar, I said to Dehan, "You got the list of students there?"

"Uh-huh."

"Bring it in with you. I want to show it to Rafa. I keep going over this. She was killed by somebody she knew, who wasn't there." I pulled up outside the bar, killed the engine, and yanked up the handbrake. "That's wrong, right?"

She smiled and opened the door. "It *was* Halloween, Sensei!"

Rafa was about ten years older than me. He was sitting at the bar with a beer between his forearms, watching reruns of old games and popping peanuts into his mouth. He had a shiny, bald head with long, scraggly hair that hung from his ears to his shoulder blades. When we stepped in, he turned, smiled, jumped down from his stool, and embraced me and slapped my back like we were old buddies. He shook Dehan's hand and kissed her on the cheek. Then he grabbed his drink and he and Dehan moved to a table. I ordered a couple of beers and joined them.

"So," Rafa said, grinning, "you two, huh? Who'd'a thunk it?" He laughed. "No, I'm really happy for you guys." He leaned toward Dehan and gestured at me. "I don't know how you put up with this arrogant SOB, but I am glad for you!"

Dehan gave a small, dry laugh. "You'll say the same to him as soon as I go to the john."

We gave the obligatory laugh, and with the preliminaries out of the way, I said, "Listen, Rafa, you know we're working the cold cases, right?"

"Yeah, I heard you're putting everybody to shame—again."

I shook my head. "Not at all. Cases go cold for very good

reasons. You look at them again with fresh eyes and notice different things. You know that."

"Sure I do. I'm just messing with you." He sat back in his chair with realization dawning on his face. "Ooh . . . So let me guess. You're reopening the Sue Benedict case?"

"Yup."

"Man! After twelve years? I wish you luck. You know me, right? I mean, we were never pals . . ." He turned to Dehan. "Stone and me, we was never like close pals, you know? But he knew me, and . . ." He turned back to me. "You know I would never drop a case unless there was just zero evidence, right?"

I nodded. "I know that, Rafa, and that's kind of why we're here. So far we have three witnesses, for want of a better word. We've Juan at the church, Giorgio, who is a royal pain in the ass and about as useful as a footbrake on a wheelchair, and Fernando, who we haven't spoken to yet, but I'm willing to bet he's going to be about as useful as his pal Giorgio."

Dehan had narrowed her eyes and was shaking her head at me. I knew why and I didn't care.

"Seriously? A footbrake on a wheelchair? You said that?"

Rafa was wheezing a laugh. "Yeah, twelve years ago and you brought it right back. You ask him any damned question and he'd answer by telling you what kind of an artist he was: 'I did not notice, Detective, because me, I am an artist of the soul . . .'"

I laughed. "That's about it. What was your take on the case, Rafa? Did you have any suspects?"

He watched Dehan pull out the list of students and slide them across the table. He shook his head. "Jeez, buy a girl a drink, guys! If you'd given me some warning, I could have refreshed my memory."

He looked over the names, leaned back in his chair, and stared at the TV for a while. Then he started talking while still looking at the TV.

"Things I remember, we went through all the guests, who were pretty much everyone on that list . . ." He paused and looked at me. "You'd know this if you bothered to read the damned report."

I smiled without feeling. "But you have such a nice speaking voice, I like to hear it from you."

"Yeah, right. So we worked our way through them and they all alibied each other, plus we couldn't find anybody with any kind of issue with Sue. But . . ." He reached out and turned his glass around three times. "There were three exceptions to what I am saying: there was Giorgio, who disappeared from the party around two thirty. He says he went up to his bedroom with three women . . ."

"Rocio, Karen, and Ruby."

"Correct."

Dehan had picked up the list of names and was going through them. Rafa said, "You won't find them on the list. They weren't in the group, and they weren't invited to the party. When we challenged him about that, he admitted they were prostitutes and he had called them. He couldn't remember the number."

Dehan asked, "You checked his phone records?"

He shook his head. "By that time, we had the DNA and fingerprints from the lab. Everybody at the party gave us a sample and they were all cleared, including Giorgio. We had no justifiable reason for checking whether he had been with those prostitutes or not."

She grunted, and Rafa went on. "Same thing with Fernando. He said he left with Sue, she told him she didn't want to sleep with him, he went his way, and she went hers. But there is a witness you might want to talk to . . ."

Dehan said, "Patterson Avenue."

"So you *did* at least glance at the report. Yeah, just across the road from Sue. He saw a man matching Fernando's description going up the stairs to Sue's place with her. He said they had a brief scuffle. He went to get the phone to call 911, but when he got back to the window, the man was walking away and the door was closed. Next thing, he saw another man approach and climb the stairs: short to medium height, woolen hat, pretty much nondescript. He saw the door open, the guy stood there for a moment and then went in."

"Could it have been Fernando, come back?"

"That's what I asked. The witness said it was possible, but he didn't think so."

I sipped my beer. "You said there were three exceptions: Giorgio, Fernando, and . . . ?"

"Cyril Browne, with an *e*. My understanding is that he was at the party, though just about none of the people who were there remembered him. Those who did varied from being sure they saw him to thinking they might have seen him. Apparently he's the kind of guy who sits in the corner and nobody knows he's there."

I was surprised and my face said so. "And Cyril was one of Giorgio's students?"

"Yup, and apparently he was pretty good. But in class it was the same as at the party, nobody was ever sure if he was there or not. He never got involved, never spoke to anybody, shy, insecure, whatever. So he was probably at the party, but we can't be one hundred percent sure."

Dehan had been listening with her glass halfway to her mouth. Now she put it down without drinking and said, "Okay, so I am going to ask the stupid question. Why didn't you ask him?"

"He vanished."

Dehan made a face like three Os.

Rafa looked at me and said, "It's in the report."

"We only picked up the case this morning, Rafa. We'll read and digest tonight. Meantime, help me out. What do you mean, he vanished?"

"We went to his house, he wasn't there. We contacted his landlord, he'd given two months' notice end of August, and had left November first."

"The day after the party. That is one hell of a coincidence."

"Tell me about it. Naturally, Giorgio and Fernando were no

longer suspects. Aside from the fact that their DNA didn't match, this guy's behavior obviously made him the prime suspect."

Dehan was nodding. "Did you manage to trace him at all?"

"Kinda. We discovered he had a sister in California. I'm not being funny, but the address is in the file. Elk Grove, if I remember right, in Sacramento. We called her, and she said she hadn't heard from Cyril in years. She said she'd let us know if he turned up. We put out a BOLO." He shrugged and pulled a face. "But it was like he'd vanished off the face of the Earth. We even got a court order to try and recover genetic material from the house, but he'd got professional cleaners in and there was not a trace of him anywhere."

For a moment, he looked embarrassed. "There wasn't a lot more we could do. We canvassed his workmates—he was a librarian—to see if there was anybody who might be hiding him, but the universal consensus was that he was a bit weird, a loner, had no friends, and kept to himself. He'd handed in his notice two months earlier there too, at the same time he handed in his notice to his landlord. Didn't say where he was going, something vague about going abroad."

I called for another round of beers and scratched my head. "So, two months earlier, he decides to kill Sue on Halloween. I get the feeling he is a meticulous planner. He hands in his notice at work and with his landlord, comes along to the Halloween party, and when she leaves, he follows . . ." I paused and shook my head. "I have a couple of problems with this scenario. First, if he is such a meticulous planner, why does he pick a method of killing her that he cannot be a hundred percent sure will work? He can't guarantee she will be alone that night. She might have spent the night with Giorgio or Fernando. Also, even if she was alone, how can he be sure that she will let him in?"

Rafa shrugged. "I'd love to have asked him." Then he suddenly made a face like mental constipation.

Dehan was watching him and nodding like she was reading his constipated mind. She said, "I don't think he's the guy."

Rafa nodded at her.

I said, "What makes you say that?"

The barman came over with a tray of beer and set them in front of us on the table. When he went away, Dehan said, "Okay, this is going to sound crazy, but hear me out. Everything and anything Cyril does is going to look weird and creepy, because the one thing this guy does not want is for anybody ever to notice him. Right?"

Rafa was nodding, staring at his beer. "That's exactly what I think."

I said, "Okay."

"So, the only reason it looks weird that he gave notice at work and to his landlord is because he didn't tell anybody about it. Anybody else would have told his workmates, his family, friends . . . But Cyril is a loner and he doesn't tell anybody. He just goes. So it looks like he's on the run. But aside from the coincidence of dates, there is nothing that points to him as her rapist or her killer."

"Disappearing after a murder is fairly strong circumstantial evidence."

"But did he do a runner?" She raised her eyebrows. "He gave two months' notice. That's not much of a runner. Plus, as you yourself said, the rape has the feel of being opportunistic, not planned. This guy seems to be a planner, not an opportunist."

I grunted. "There is also the small fact of the DNA. He is the only person at the party whose DNA was not tested." I took a long pull and looked at them both. "If not him, who?"

Rafa nodded. "I have to say, Stone, I always thought it was Giorgio. It's wrong to say 'I thought.' There is very little evidence pointing to him, but I had a gut feeling."

"How do you account for the DNA?"

"I can't, but you know like I do, that's not impossible to rig."

I snorted. "Not impossible, but damned difficult."

Dehan gave me a long, skeptical look. "There were apparently three hookers at the party . . ."

I smiled. "So when everybody is good and drunk, Giorgio telephones his three hookers . . ."

Dehan took over. "Meanwhile, Fernando has left with Sue. He makes sure she gets home and returns to the party, where Cyril has been taken into a room upstairs with the hookers. It's all done in the spirit of good fun. The girls are sweet to him and make him wear a condom. Once they have the semen, either Fernando or Giorgio, or both, return, rape, and kill her and plant the evidence."

Rafa leaned back, pointing at her. "I like that theory better than Cyril. It's convoluted because it has to be, but it makes more sense to me as a cop than this little guy planning an opportunistic murder two months ahead. You said yourself, Stone, it makes no sense to plan everything ahead and leave the actual kill to chance."

Dehan's face was almost apologetic. "I have to say I agree. Cyril just doesn't ring true."

I turned it over and around in my head a few times, then asked Rafa, "Anything else?"

He thought for a moment, with his arms crossed, then said, "Basically, Stone, the way I see it, you have three or four options, depending how you look at it. One, like I just said, Cyril planned this murder for at least two months, but left the actual killing to chance; two, and maybe three, Giorgio and/or Fernando killed her and framed Cyril; three, or four, it was opportunistic. Some guy passing saw her go in, saw she was drunk, rang at the door, and pushed his way in."

Dehan drained her glass and tried and failed to repress a belch. "That is in many ways the most likely scenario, but the big drawback is that an opportunist who manages to rape and kill a woman without upsetting any furniture is statistically very likely to have a rap sheet. And this guy did not show up on any database."

Rafa shrugged again. "Which leaves you back with Giorgio or Fernando. Motive would not be impossible to find. By the looks of it, they were into her, but she was not into them. MO? What your partner said. A frame-up."

I gave something like a reluctant nod. "Food for thought."

"I'm sorry I couldn't be more helpful." With a hint of irony, he added, "If I could'a been, I would probably have solved it myself."

I laughed. "Sure. I hear you."

We stood and shook hands, thanked him for his time, and stepped out into the freezing dusk, where the streetlamps and shop fronts were already beginning to light up, and the clouded sky above was turning dark.

"So what now, Sensei?"

I leaned on the roof of the Jag and shuddered. "Now, you get on the phone and request Cyril Browne's financials from the end of August 2006. While you do that, I'm going to phone Frank. Then we go and visit Fernando. We'll see if he's as much of a pain in the ass as his friend Giorgio."

We climbed in the car out of the cold and slammed the doors.

Scan the QR code below to purchase TRICK OR TREAT.
Or go to: righthouse.com/trick-or-treat

Printed in Great Britain
by Amazon